LOVE LETTERS

STARLING BAY BOOK 3

SIENNA CARR

Author's Note

~

Love Letters is a STANDALONE romance. It is the 3rd book in the ***Starling Bay*** series. While you do not need to have read the first two books, ***Winter's Kiss***, or, **Maid for Him**, it might enhance your reading experience if you do, because many of the characters in this book appear in the other Starling Bay books.

Starling Bay Series:

Whirlwind Kisses
Winter's Kiss
Maid for Him
Love Letters
Escape to Starling Bay (Books 1-3)
From Faking to Forever
Winter's Vow
Guarded Hearts
Table for Two
A Bouquet of Charm
Christmas Hope

Newsletter sign up: http://www.siennacarr.com/newsletter

"I never expected that, did you?" Rourke asked his friend Dylan, as their friend Reed walked away towards his car.

"It's not that surprising." Dylan checked his cell phone for the umpteenth time.

Rourke and his friends had just left the Blue Velvet Bar where Reed had dropped a huge bombshell; not about his engagement breaking up—he'd told them about that a few weeks ago when he'd hinted that his then fiancée, Olivia, had blamed his maid, Jenna, for the break-up. Reed had explained that his and Olivia's problems had started soon after they got engaged. But *still,* even though the break-up had been a shock, it had been nothing compared to tonight's news: that Jenna no longer worked for Reed, and, even more shocking, he had hinted of an attraction between them.

Reed had kept it vague, as was to be expected of a man like him. But the news had shocked Rourke; not so much because Jenna had been Reed's maid, but more because, up until tonight, Rourke had suspected that Jenna might have been the one sending love notes. He'd received three now, and the third one only a few days ago. They had started on Valentine's Day with each subsequent one arriving two weeks later.

He didn't know what to make of it.

"What do you mean it's not surprising?" Rourke growled. Dylan acted like a know-it-all most of the time, and acted as if most things didn't surprise him. Rourke didn't care what this smart aleck said this time. Reed and Jenna getting together was big news.

Dylan was still texting, and had a goofy smile on his face.

"Texting Merry again?" Rourke groaned. "I'm still here and trying to have a conversation with you." He clicked his fingers.

"Just letting her know I'll be back in half an hour," his friend replied.

"Why?"

Dylan looked up at him, stopped texting and put the phone away. "Because … why not? Why are you so grouchy?"

Rourke folded his arms. "Reed's news is a shock, that's all."

"It wasn't that big of a shock. I saw that coming."

"Even after the ball?"

"Especially after the ball."

"Were you and I at the same ball?" Rourke asked, because he'd seen Reed go up on stage, had seen his fiancée look stunning in that red dress, and they'd both looked like a couple in love. They'd kissed on the stage. They'd looked happy. What had he missed? "What did you see that I didn't see?"

Dylan sighed. "It was there all along. Don't you pay attention to anything?"

Rourke opened his mouth to say something, but didn't. He *did* pay attention. Mostly to women. He could scan a room within seconds of stepping into it and filter out the lookers in one glance.

"But Jenna?" he asked. That had come as a surprise. Most men had a type. He had his. His ideal woman was slim, feminine and beautiful. Of course, it could be any number of women in

Starling Bay who matched that description, and it was eating him up trying to figure out who it could be that was sending the notes.

He preferred women with long hair, and a tall, slender figure. Leggy, too. He loved long, long, long legs. He'd been using his type, and interactions with the women he knew, to narrow down his list of possible senders of the love notes.

Jenna was, well…pretty, but she was also different. Her blue hair put her in the slightly crazy category. He didn't think she was Reed's type either, but maybe a man's *real* type versus the imagined type diverged in reality.

The only reason he'd considered Jenna as a possible sender had been because the love notes had started arriving soon after she returned to Starling Bay. This was why he'd been so interested in her for the past couple of months.

And they'd gone to the same school many, many years ago. He figured it had to be someone he knew, even someone from his past. At least he hoped so. The idea of a random stalker being behind the love notes scared the heck out of him.

"What's that supposed to mean?" Dylan asked as he walked towards his pickup. Rourke followed. "She's not his type."

"Maybe she is now," said Dylan. "Or do you mean about her being a maid? Who cares about that stuff? Jenna seems like a nice person, from the little I saw of her at the ball. I don't know her. Thing is, it doesn't matter what we think of her. Reed likes her, and we've got to be there for him."

"Yeah, of course. We do," Rourke agreed, "But he's a dark horse."

"Talking of dark horses, are you really not going to celebrate your birthday? Or do you have secret plans with a secret girlfriend?" Dylan asked.

"I don't have a girlfriend right now."

"And you're definitely not celebrating your birthday at all?"

"No, and I don't want to keep telling you guys that."

"Touchy."

"It's just another birthday." He didn't want a fuss; he didn't want a celebration with a big party. His parents had come over last weekend, and they'd gone to Fellini's for dinner. The popular Italian restaurant was a family favorite. Too bad his sister, Shelly, hadn't been able to make it. He'd told her it was no big deal, but she thought he was in denial, and that he was possibly going through a mid-life crisis twenty years early.

He disagreed. He was fine. Turning thirty was no big deal. No big deal at all.

"It is another birthday, you're right," Dylan agreed. "After a while, it doesn't matter and the numbers don't mean jack."

Rourke sniggered. "Of course you're going to say that because you're positively ancient, pal."

"My age doesn't bother me as much as turning thirty bothers you, *pal*. See you soon?"

"I'm always free," Rourke replied easily. "I should ask if you and Reed have time for me these days, seeing that you're both busy with your new love interests."

"You're definitely grumpy tonight. Call me when you're in a better mood." Dylan winked at him and drove away.

Maybe he was a little peeved that he could no longer claim he was in his twenties, but other than that, he was fine.

Other than this irritating little thing he now had to deal with. He walked towards his car, doubly perplexed because the mystery had suddenly deepened. He climbed into his seat and pulled the most recent notecard out of his jacket pocket.

Just like the two before it, this notecard had also been delivered to his work address. It was a pretty little card, white with colored flowers on the front. Each of the three cards had pictures of flowers, and this one also had little pink hearts.

A girlie card.

There was no printed writing inside, only a handwritten poem. This third one said:

If I were brave, I would shine a beam,
And light up your path to me.
There's no other way to make you see,
That you and I were meant to be.

The first one had been unexpected and a nice surprise. The second one had been interesting, and still a nice surprise. This third one had been a pleasant distraction from work, from turning thirty, and from his very-much-single status. It had been an uplifting boost when he'd believed that Jenna might have been a contender, when he'd thought he could pin a face to the person behind it. But now that Reed had hinted, albeit vaguely, of an attraction between him and Jenna, this line of enquiry was out of the question.

He shoved the note back into his pocket. In the general scheme of things, of life, and the new hire at work, and the properties he was working on selling, these love notes weren't important. But they were a minor irritation. Who the heck was sending them and how long was he supposed to put up with receiving them?

With Jenna out of the equation now, it could be any number of women. He was going to have a hard time figuring out exactly who.

CHAPTER 2

"*H*ey."

Daisy, the cute little receptionist, blazed her full-watt smile at him as he walked past.

"Hey," he flashed the smile back, grabbed one of the newspapers from the coffee table, and returned to his office. The same thought gnawed away at him.

Could she be the one?

Daisy was too young. Way too young. Though maybe it was the type of thing someone this young would do.

He didn't like the idea of a work colleague being attracted to him. He always kept his work life and his romantic life separate. It was precisely for this reason that Daisy hadn't caught his attention even though she was pretty enough. She had the long flowing locks that he liked, and a pretty face, if not the height and long limbs that usually caught his attention.

Those darned love notes, notecards or whatever they were, were going to drive him to a slow death if he wasn't careful. He couldn't walk past a woman these days without wondering if she might have been the one who'd sent them.

He opened the newspaper and glanced through it quickly.

Across from him at the other end of the room was Angelo, talking on the phone to a client. A new hire who had only joined Dyson Realty a few months ago, Angelo often reminded Rourke of himself, albeit a much younger version of himself. The guy was good, if a little overconfident, but being a salesman required that kind of bravado, and Angelo had that in abundance.

In fact, Rourke had a meeting with Dyson later today to make a final decision about taking Angelo on full-time.

He glanced at the newspaper again but nothing was really sinking in because his mind was still on those darned love notes. It was annoying because he had no idea who they were from, and therefore he had no control over the situation. He liked to be in control and these blasted notes made him feel helpless. And to make matters worse, he now viewed all his interactions with women with a degree of suspicion.

"Are you going out to get some lunch?" Angelo asked him, as he hung up the phone.

Rourke looked up. "Lunch?" Was it that time of day already? Lunch was a great idea. He felt cooped up sitting inside the office. "Sure." He rose. "Aren't you coming?"

"Can't," Angelo replied. "I've got a two o'clock with Dyson. He wants to know what I think of the place. Got any tips?"

Rourke put his hands into his slacks pockets. "You'll do fine. Just tell him what you like about the job, and what you don't like."

"There's nothing I don't like," Angelo replied. "I want to work here permanently."

"Then tell him." Rourke slipped on his jacket. "Want me to get you anything?"

Angelo shook his head. "I was going to ask you to get me a pastrami sandwich from Roxy's but I've kind of lost my appetite."

"You're nervous?" He grinned in surprise. "I didn't think that being nervous was in your DNA. Just tell Tony the truth," he said. "You'll be fine."

He'd put in a good word for the kid. He'd found him quick, and bright, and eager to learn. And he was a charmer. Could talk to women, had a natural affinity for making quick and easy conversation, pretty much like Rourke did. Except the kid wasn't even in his mid-twenties yet.

Annoyed with the reminder about age, he left the office, eager for a breath of fresh air. Plus, he wasn't going to find out who the mysterious note sender was by sitting at his desk all day. It was time to turn detective.

He stepped into Roxy's Diner, and it must have been his lucky day because the owner was actually at the counter today. Roxy didn't always work on the counters now that she'd taken on staff. Her parents had worked here for years, with Roxy and her brother, Jackson, helping out during the holidays and on weekends. Now it belonged to Roxy.

"Hey, Rox." He smiled, looking for a flicker of recognition, a sign, a giveaway.

"Hey yourself," she replied. "It's a little early for you today, isn't it?"

She had noticed. That alerted him. "I'm extra hungry today, plus I'm getting an order for my friend."

"What can I get you today? Chicken salad no dressing?"

How did she know about that? He'd only recently started to have chicken salad for lunch. "Am I that predictable?"

"Not really. You're always full of surprises, Rourke," she said, tempting him as she rearranged the breaded chicken breast filets on the serving tray in the display counter. "You liked these before, didn't you? Gone off them now?"

She *had* noticed. Breaded cheesy parmesan chicken filets inside a ciabatta roll had been his go-to on most days, but he'd been forced to put a hold on them after seeing his stomach start to sag. Not a good look for a thirty-something man who had yet to meet the woman of his dreams.

"No. They're still pretty good. I just have to watch my waistline."

"Oh, puh-leese," she laughed, shaking her head while her gaze dipped down to his waistline. "Don't go giving me that excuse."

"It's true," he said, tapping his stomach. He and Roxy had double-dated a few times almost a decade ago, when her friend and his friend, who were going steady at the time, had suggested it. He'd vaguely known her from school prior to that though they hadn't mixed in the same friend circles. While the double-dating had been a disaster, afterwards, they had somehow become friends.

Maybe she was interested in him again, and maybe sending the note cards was her way of testing the waters?

He was tempted to ask her outright, after all, they had that sort of camaraderie, but what if he was wrong? Roxy would never let him forget it. "You have a good memory," he told her. "Remembering everyone's orders."

"It comes with the job. You get to know people, and what they like."

The handwriting. All he needed was a sample of her handwriting and he would know for sure. He tried to read her expression, tried to see if there was a tell-tale look in those eyes. There wasn't. Roxy looked at him as if she was bored waiting for him to make up his mind.

"I'll have a chicken salad without the dressing, a pastrami sandwich for my friend, and two bottles of water to go, please."

"Coming right up," she said, doing her magic and putting everything together at lightning speed.

"Could you…" he faltered, knowing it sounded dumb. "Could

you write down your details." He tried to think. "For a…a party I'm having."

A party? He blinked at his own stupidity. Why the heck had he gone and said that?

"A party?"

"Yeah, uh, could you give me some pricing details?" He said the first thing he thought of.

"Pricing details?" Roxy fixed his chicken salad in a plastic container, grabbed two bottles of water and put them into a bag for him along with the sandwich. She told him the price, then asked, "How many people at your party?"

He handed her a twenty-dollar bill. "Ten… maybe thirty."

"Ten, maybe *thirty?*" She handed him back the change.

"I'm not sure yet."

"What's the occasion?"

Darn it. "No major reason. It was my birthday a week ago and—"

"Oh! Well, in that case, Happy Birthday, Rourke. The big thirty, am I right?"

"You're right. So, I was thinking I should do something."

"It's your thirtieth, of course you've got to do something."

"So, if you could jot down some details of the potential cost, as in the cost per head, or however you do it, that would be great. Just give me a ballpark figure for thirty people." Thirty people for a party he wasn't having, to celebrate a new age bracket he'd suddenly slipped into? No way. But this was insane, and all in the name of getting Roxy's handwriting.

She handed him a brochure. "This has everything you need, but we can discuss the menu when you're ready. I need to know what type of food you want me to serve. Do you want vegetarian, or meats, and if so, which? Pasta and salad, if so, what types. Do you want canapés? It's all in here." She nodded at the brochure she'd handed him. "This is a relatively new venture for me, catering for parties, so I can't price it off the top of my head, and it would help me to know when it's for so that I can make a booking for you."

"Let me think about it, and I'll ..uh…I'll get back to you. Do you have a number, maybe you could jot down your phone number and a contact email address or something, Rox?"

"Here," she handed him a business card. "That has everything you need."

His face fell flat. She was doing everything she could to avoid giving him her handwriting. That had to be a sign. "Thanks, Rox. I'll let you know."

On the way back from Roxy's, he walked past the florist's shop. Her small van was parked on the narrow street outside. The name BLOOM emblazoned in bright pink letters against a black background. She came out, and smiled at him, before locking her vehicle. "Did I miss you?" she asked, as he stopped in his tracks. He'd bought flowers from here on many occasions and had spoken to the new owner a few times, but he didn't know her too well.

When he looked puzzled by her question, she said, "Sorry, I usually never close the shop during the day but I had to rush over to The Grand Hotel to drop off some flowers for a convention."

"Oh, I…I was just admiring your displays."

"So I didn't miss you?"

"No."

Her smile widened. "Good! I got worried there for a moment."

She walked into her shop, and he followed. The brightly colored bunches of flowers on display caught his attention and lured him in. "Your flower displays are stunning," he told her and gave her one of his best smiles.

"Thank you. I can't complain about my view of the office."

They both laughed. After a few seconds, she asked him, "Are you just looking or buying today?"

"Uh…" He wasn't one to be stuck on what to say but she'd never asked him before, and the fact that she had now made him wonder, and look deeper, trying to find meaning in her words. "I'm not sure," he confessed.

"You don't usually buy until after work."

Another one who had noticed. He marked her down as a definite possibility in his head, before glancing at the table in one corner at the back. It looked like she made up her bouquets and flower arrangements there.

"I was only passing by," he said, not particularly looking to buy anything. He didn't have anyone to buy flowers for at the moment. This was taxing, being admired and not having a darn clue by whom. "Just looking, for now." He stopped over by the bucket of carnations.

"Take as long as you want. I'll be over in the corner."

"Thanks. I don't think we've been properly introduced before," he said.

"Mackenzie," she said, holding out her hand. "Mackenzie Jeffers."

"Mackenzie," he said, shaking her hand gently. "That's an unusual name."

"Thank you, I think."

"Oh, it's a compliment. Definitely a compliment."

Could she be the one?

"And you are?" she asked, turning her face towards him. He couldn't help but notice her long and slender neck.

"Rourke. Rourke Halloran." Just then he glimpsed, lying on the table, a couple of cards, bigger than the ones he'd received, but he could make out that they had sketches of flowers on them.

Could it be a coincidence?

Probably.

But what if it wasn't?

"Now, that's an unusual name," she said, interrupting his thoughts.

He turned and looked at her again. "Yes, yes, it is. My mom said she loved the name. It belonged to one of her favorite characters in some long-running romance and mystery series. Mine's spelled differently, apparently."

"Interesting," she replied, giving him another beautiful smile and making him pay attention.

This was the longest conversation he'd ever had with her, and he hadn't even bought anything. Could her interest be a sign, or a clue that it was her?

He tried to think of a way he could get a sample of her handwriting, but before he could ask her for anything, his cell phone rang. "Excuse me." He moved away to take the call. It was Angelo.

"Where are you?" he asked. "Dyson's waiting for you. He said you were meant to be in on the second half of the meeting."

He'd forgotten completely.

Darn.

It had slipped his mind. This was what happened when things like those pesky little love notes clouded his thinking. "I'm on my way."

"Did you get my lunch?" Angelo asked.

"Yes, I got your lunch."

He turned to Mackenzie apologetically. "Sorry, I have to go, but I'll be back another time."

"You know where I am."

He walked out, her words still ringing in his ears, the double meaning working overtime. He'd never even considered that it could be the florist, but this had been a most interesting revelation. He now had two possibilities. Roxy and Mackenzie.

He rushed back to work, not having solved his mystery, but feeling as if he was a little closer than he had been to making a discovery. He was determined to get to the bottom of it quickly so that he could get on with things the way he had before. The love notes distraction was getting to be a serious pain in the butt.

"I'll keep this short," Dyson said as soon as Rourke walked into his manager's office after quickly scoffing his lunch. That's a relief, thought Rourke. He was getting close to selling a property and wanted to get this meeting over with.

"I've spoken with Angelo. He's happy, I'm happy, what about you? What's your recommendation?"

Rourke settled into the chair across from his boss. "He's a good addition to the team. He's a team player, he's worked on a few properties with me, and we've managed to close those deals quickly."

"I noticed." Dyson fluffed through some papers. "I like the kid."

"I like him too," Rourke agreed. Angelo Martinez was good. He was a charmer, and he seemed especially good with women. That had been Rourke's way when it came to selling houses, and if he wasn't careful, he was going to be the older, wiser realty guy to Angelo's young cool and hip one.

"Fits in?"

Rourke nodded. "He's a hard worker, and he gets on with everyone. I don't have to babysit him too much." And he could sell houses. They were in the business of selling houses, not anything else. He patted his stomach, feeling the slight bulge, evidence of his middle-age spread beginning a decade too early.

"That's what we want. Self-starters. He reminds me of you," said Dyson, rising out of his chair. "A younger version of you."

"Thanks," Rourke replied, his ego deflated. Turning thirty

seemed to have changed people's perception of him. He also noticed that where he once used to be one of the young ones around, even here, in Dyson's company, he was no longer the youngest of them all.

Mirror, mirror on the wall…

"Get Phil to move into your office so that Phil can work with Angelo now, and you can move into the office next to mine."

"Is that a metaphor for a promotion?" he asked, grinning.

"No. It's just you moving into another office," replied Dyson, without blinking an eye. It wasn't the answer Rourke wanted. He'd been here for years, ever since leaving college, and he was the top salesman consistently. It was high time Dyson recognized that and gave him a promotion.

"You seem distracted lately," Dyson continued. "Everything okay?"

The comment stung, but Rourke tried not to show his displeasure. "Yes."

"Good, because a multi-million dollar property in Glassmere has just come on the market and the owner obviously wants the full asking price."

Rourke gasped loudly.

Glassmere. Reed's neck of the woods. Properties around there rarely came on the market. The commission on that was going to be huge.

"We'll work on that together," Dyson told him. "It's going to take a lot of our time, so I suggest you bring Angelo and Phil up to speed on your existing properties."

"Will do." This was good news. Angelo as his sidekick, taking care of the smaller things, so that he could focus on the big stuff. This was further evidence that Dyson was priming him for bigger things even if he wasn't going to say it using those words. His mood suddenly lifted.

"Also," said Dyson, clearing his throat. "I'm going to be busy next week, so I need you to meet with Francine Gray from the recruitment agency. She's only coming to sign the relevant paperwork for Angelo. Make it quick; we don't want her to take up too much of your time. We're in the business of selling properties, not wasting time."

"I'll take care of it."

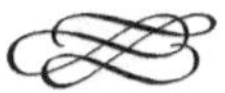

CHAPTER 3

She hadn't been sure about it. About sending them all, but now that she had written them, it made sense to send them on.

It was only supposed to have been a Valentine's Day bit of fun, but she'd gotten carried away, and decided to send a few more and mailed them two weeks apart.

She wasn't there when he received them, and she often wondered what his reaction would be.

He would never suspect.

Never.

She'd written the fourth note and slipped it into the envelope, sealed it and put it to the side, ready to mail to him tomorrow.

No more, she thought. Well, maybe the last one. And then no more.

One day she might get the courage to own up to her bit of fun, but she wasn't ready for that yet. She wasn't sure how he would take it if he knew these cards had come from her.

Because Rourke Halloran had a reputation for being a ladies' man, on the surface of it, but she knew underneath it all he was sweet and kind, and that he had a soft heart.

CHAPTER 4

His eyelids flew open and he gasped. But the sight of his familiar ceiling calmed him.

He was fine. He felt around, could feel his toes, and his fingers.

It had only been a bad dream, a woman chasing him through a park, but it had just been a dream.

Thank goodness he didn't have a rabbit for a pet. He'd felt like the man in a movie he'd seen, where the psycho woman boiled his bunny.

"This is crazy," Rourke mumbled, getting out of bed and jumping into the shower. Going by the timelines of the other love notes, he was due to receive another one soon in a few days' time and he was obviously getting tetchy thinking about it.

It was going to drive him nuts, whether it arrived or not.

A man like him was used to controlling the situation, especially when it came to women and asking them on a date. He initiated the flirting, he called them, and he did the chasing. Often, a woman would flirt back, would reveal her interest and then it was even easier.

The ticking clock of his next love note, if indeed there was to be another one, had him worried and he'd gone to bed with the thought of it hanging over him.

It was an anxiety as unfamiliar as it was unwanted. He wasn't used to being chased. *He* did the chasing, he was the one who hit on women he found attractive. But now that the tables were turned, now that he was the one being preyed upon, he didn't like it. Nor did he know how to handle it. Getting hit on was bad enough, but getting hit on by a nameless, faceless woman was even worse.

What if she was a stalker? What if it was someone he had wronged, or dumped? What if this woman was now trying to lull him into a false sense of security, by making him think that she was nice and attracted to him, when in reality, her real goal might be to get revenge? What if she wanted to hurt him? A real psycho would think like that.

These were the places his mind had started to wander to lately.

Or what if she was nice, and sweet, and normal, but she wasn't his type? What if she wasn't attractive? He needed to speak to someone about it, but who? It was hardly something he wanted to broach with Angelo, a guy he didn't know well enough yet, and Reed and Dylan always seemed too busy lately. And even if they had time, he wasn't ready to talk to them about this yet, mostly for fear of being laughed at.

He went to work and had a hectic morning since Dyson was away. It wasn't until lunchtime, when he ate a sandwich at his desk, that he had time to take a breath. He had a meeting scheduled with Francine Gray, the owner of the recruitment agency. But before that, he needed his afternoon caffeine shot and sugar rush. It was time to go to his favorite shop.

He pushed the door open to Books & Buns, the cozy bookstore with a café. It was run by Leigh, his sister Shelly's best friend.

He strode straight over to the cake counter where Leigh was setting out some more cakes and pastries.

"Choices, choices, choices," he mumbled, eyeing up the selection. "What shall I have today?"

Leigh looked up and smiled. "Hey, there. It's Rourke o'clock."

"Very funny." It was a little joke between them because he often turned up here at some point during the afternoon. "No more cinnamon buns?" Disappointment rolled over him. He had grown partial to these ever since Leigh had started selling them around Christmastime.

"Sorry. Not today, but we do have those small lemon drizzle loaves that you love. I just baked a fresh batch." His face lit up at the mention of his other favorite cake.

"You're still baking?" he asked, wondering how she managed it all, running the bookshop as well as the homemade cakes.

"I only make a few cakes, the rest I buy. It's not a problem because I love to bake, so it's kind of hard to stop myself."

"I wish Shelly could bake."

"What's wrong with you learning?" Leigh asked, raising an eyebrow.

"Tastes better when someone else has made it."

"That's true."

"I'll take one of those lemon drizzle loaves," he said, pointing.

"To go?"

"No. I'll have it here, thanks, and I'll have a strong black coffee to go with that."

"Coming right up. Take a seat."

He walked over and sat a few tables away from the service counter. As far as he was concerned, a place like this beat all the chain stores. Books & Buns was definitely one of Starling Bay's hidden gems.

The walls of the café corner were adorned with pretty pictures of books and quotes from them. Leigh had done a great job with this bookstore when she'd taken it over a few years ago. It used to be a bakery but she'd transformed it into a two-story bookshop with a café on the ground floor. There were comfy sofas for reading on both levels, but he mostly preferred to sit at the tables in the cafe. He got out his folder and his notes from the brochures that they'd put together for the latest houses on the market. He also had a few contracts he needed to look over. Setting these out on the table, he soon got to work.

"Here you go," Leigh's cheery voice made him snap to attention a short while later. "Lemon drizzle and a strong black coffee." She placed his order in front of him. He looked at the little lemon drizzle loaf and made a noise as if he had difficulty deciding what to do with it. The decision had been made for him when he'd placed his order, but now that he was reminded of the calories, the doubt crept in.

"What's wrong?" Leigh asked.

"I shouldn't really be having that."

"But you like lemon drizzle."

"I do. It's one of my favorites but—"

"I can get you something else if you prefer. How about—"

He tapped his stomach. "I should be eating more salads. Less cake."

She shook her head in amazement. "You're kidding me, Rourke."

"I wish I was."

"Shelly said you were having problems adjusting."

"Adjusting with what?" His sister had given him a hard time over his reluctance not to celebrate his milestone birthday.

"Turning thirty."

He rolled his eyes. "That is not true."

"Um-hmmm," said Leigh, folding her arms. "I could make some healthier cakes and cookies."

He made a face, not liking that suggestion. "Bad idea. This is what I look forward to." He jerked his head towards the cake. "I *need* my cinnamon buns and lemon drizzle. Eh…what the heck." He ignored his earlier resolve and took a huge bite out of the cake, savoring the tangy, citrus kick, and the crunchy lemon drizzle icing. Then he washed it down with a gulp of coffee. "This is what makes my day."

"And this is what makes my day, a happy customer. Still, I like your suggestion. I'm going to give the healthier options serious consideration."

"It wasn't my suggestion," he replied, quickly. "And you don't have to go that route." He didn't want low-calorie cardboard-tasting alternatives to ruin her selection of cakes and cookies.

"I like to experiment."

"I don't know how you do it, even if you love baking. Running a bookshop can't be easy."

"I spend a lot of time here. It's my second home."

"But you do need to take it easy, Leigh. You need to take time off and you can now that you have extra staff. You'll burn out if you're not careful, Leigh."

"I know. It's been a hard slog."

"And you've done so well. Your business isn't a failure. You've made it succeed, but it will suffer if you're not feeling one hundred percent."

"So you keep telling me."

"I don't want you to get ill. I want Books & Buns to be around forever." He smiled, feeling a little sorry for her. She looked tired. "Come and sit down," he motioned, shuffling his papers to the side. Talking to Leigh took his mind off work.

"Only for a moment." She slid into the seat opposite. "I do

take weekends off, mostly. Maybe one day, but I come by the bookshop nearly every day. I can't seem to keep away."

"But you're making a profit now, right?"

She nodded. "I almost stopped believing in myself in the early days, but it's working out. It was worth the pain."

"No more pain now, right?"

"No more pain," she replied.

"Good, because I love this place. It's one of the few places I get to relax."

Her grin turned wider. "Aww, that's sweet of you to say."

"I mean it. You've done wonders with this place."

"Thank you."

"Your boyfriend must be proud of you now that you've proved him wrong." She'd mentioned in the past that he had his doubts especially when she was losing more money than she was making.

She shrugged. "I told him I would show him, and I have. He couldn't be more proud. The extra funding obviously helped. Thanks for that."

She always thanked him, even now months later, for the great deal he was able to secure for her when she'd wanted to get extra funding to have the café corner totally refurbished. He'd secured a good deal from one of Reed's contacts.

He smiled. "Don't mention it. I spend so much time in this place, the refurb has benefitted me."

She laughed. "True."

A toddler shrieked in delight a few tables away from them.

"Anytime you and your boyfriend get serious and start looking for an apartment to buy, you know where to come."

"We can't afford the types of properties you're selling, and besides, he has to put a ring on my finger first."

"Smart girl." He finished off the entire loaf. "Don't commit to anything until he commits to you first. We have all different price ranges, Leigh. I'd find you a palace within your budget."

Leigh chortled. "You're always the salesman." She looked over his shoulder at the serving counter where some customers now hovered. "I'll leave you in peace," she said, getting up and swiftly picking up an empty coffee cup from the adjoining table.

At that very moment the toddler hurtled past them, knocking Rourke's stash of papers to the floor. The child's mother rushed to grab him by the reins. "Sorry," she said, looking high-strung, as she bent down to retrieve the papers.

"Don't worry about that," said Leigh, crouching down to pick up the papers.

"He has so much energy, I don't know how to keep up with him," the mother said, as her boisterous boy tried to escape from her clutches again.

"We've got this," said Rourke, bending down and grinning as the child scooted past two tables and his mother followed. He obviously thought it was a game.

Leigh handed him the pile of papers.

"Thanks."

"Oh. Here's another one." She bent down again to retrieve it, then handed him a notecard which had fallen out. He'd forgotten that it was in there.

"Pretty," she said, handing it back to him.

"Yeah." He plucked it from her fingers quickly then glanced at his watch. "I should get back before Dyson sends out a search party for me."

CHAPTER 5

"Francine Gray from the recruitment agency is here," Daisy announced.

"I'll come out and get her." He hung up, picked up his folder and strode over to the reception area to meet with the woman. He'd never met her before, since Tony always dealt with the agency. But as he clapped eyes on the smartly dressed woman with the slicked back high ponytail and glasses, she looked vaguely familiar. She got up and offered her hand. "Hi, I'm Shay. Francine sends her apologies. She's out of town taking a course and she sent me instead."

He quirked an eyebrow. "Shay?" he asked, trying to place her.

"Shay Donovan."

"Delighted to meet you, Shay. Let's go to the conference room, shall we?" He knew who she was, and the sheer coincidence of it blew his mind away.

They sat across one another around the glass table.

"Francine's away?" he asked, making small talk.

"She's at a course."

"Tony's meeting clients."

They looked at one another and smiled.

"I know you," he said.

"We went to school together. I remember you, Rourke." A subtle smile played across her lips. She obviously knew him. An uneasy memory fluttered around in his head, making him cringe. This was *that* Shay, Jenna's friend. And now that Jenna and Reed were together, chances were high that Shay and Jenna might have discussed *that* event, the party at Reed's house where he and some of their friends had behaved deplorably and hadn't let Shay, Jenna and their friends through the door even though Reed had invited them to his party. He forced a smile. "I'm sorry for that 'incident'," he said, taking the initiative and owning up to his guilt.

She waved her hand as if dismissing his concerns. "School was a long time ago; don't worry about it."

Now that she was in front of him, he recalled having seen Shay around town over the years, but their paths had never really crossed. It seemed odd to see her properly now, face-to-face across the table, despite them both having been in Starling Bay all that time, at least, he assumed that she had been here.

It got him thinking again and his brain switched into detective mode. He'd been so busy thinking about Jenna, but could Shay be the one who had been sending the love notes? It would tie in with his theory about the love notes starting up only a few months ago, around the time Jenna had returned to Starling Bay.

He was getting ready to make more small talk, specifically to do with both their friends, Reed and Jenna, when Shay went straight to business. "Angelo Martinez," she said, pushing up her glasses, and opening her folder. "Francine told me that Mr. Dyson was eager to take him on."

"We are eager, yes. Angelo has made an excellent impression on us, and now that the three-month probationary period is over, we'd like to hire him full-time."

"Of course, you'll still be required to pay us a small

percentage of fees for the next six months, for finding such an ideal candidate."

He smiled. "Nothing's free these days, is it?"

She got out her pen. "No."

They talked about contracts and the conditions of his hire, and about the fees involved. Then they summoned Angelo in, and had a chat with him.

After Angelo signed and left, it was just Rourke and Shay in the meeting once more. At least he now had her signature on the form so that he could compare the handwriting style later.

He was being ridiculous, thinking that Shay might have had something to do with the love notes. He was slowly becoming obsessed in his quest to find the woman behind them, and if he wasn't careful, he would end up looking silly.

He tried to think of something to say, but everything he could think of, not knowing Shay too well, seemed cheesy, or forced. "I didn't recognize Jenna right away," he said, finally finding common ground, "especially with her blue hair."

"She left Starling Bay before we graduated."

"That's what I remember."

"Have you always been here?" Shay asked him.

"Always. I love this place, and my boss, Tony, has been good to me."

"Dyson Realty has been around for a while," Shay agreed. "We've placed the odd student here over the summer, for temporary placements, but Angelo is our first permanent placement."

"He's a great find," Rourke agreed. They were tiptoeing around the edges of a polite conversation that wasn't going anywhere. He didn't want to talk about business, he wanted to talk about her, and their past. Seeing her so unexpectedly, he was reminded of the teenage girl he remembered. She'd worn glasses even back then, but somehow, whether it was her high ponytail, or her lipstick, or her sharp business suit, he was seeing the woman, sexy and professional, and finding himself wondering, and partly wishing, that it might be her. His brain scrambled for something to say, for a way to have more time with her.

But she rose to standing. "Well, it was nice seeing you again, but I should get back." She held out her hand. He shook it, and stared straight into her brown eyes, trying to plumb their depths and find the secret he was searching for. He opened his mouth, considered asking her if she wanted to go for a drink at the Blue Velvet Bar, and to talk about the business there. There was no other business to talk about, they were hiring Angelo and the papers had been signed, but this line would have been enough to get him a drink with a desirable woman.

Only, he found himself hesitating.

"Nice to see you again, Shay. Maybe see you around?" He let go of her hand. "I mean, you never know with Reed and Jenna getting together."

Her beautiful lips, with a pale pink stain of lipstick, curved into a smile. "You never know."

As soon as she left, he returned to his desk, and whipped out one of the love notes to compare the handwriting on the form Shay had signed.

It was hard to see. Hard to tell with that huge flourish over the 'S' of her initial, and the rest of her name. It wasn't a definite match, nor was it completely different. It wasn't enough. A signature wasn't the best way to compare the handwriting, and he kicked himself for not getting a proper sample.

"All good?" Angelo asked.

"What?" Rourke looked up to find his colleague staring at him expectantly.

"Did something go wrong, because you look all serious?"

Rourke released a laugh. The kid looked so worried. "No. Everything's cool. You're hired."

"You had me worried."

Rourke sat back in the chair, let his shoulders slump when he realized he'd been so tense, and so desperate to find a handwriting match.

"Something else came up, something urgent. Sorry, I didn't mean to scare the heck out of you."

Angelo looked relieved.

But Rourke started to think about Shay and whether she might be the one. He was starting to hate this. Every conversation or meeting he had with a woman these days, even a relative stranger, had him obsessing over whether it could be her.

He wished whoever it was would reveal herself and put him out of his misery.

CHAPTER 6

Grab it while I can, the things that matter,
the feels, the smiles that set my heart a flutter,
Grab it while I can, while I still have time,
while I pretend, and make-believe that one day you
could be mine.

Those had been the lines from today's poem. He glanced at it while Dylan had gone to the washroom.

He was calling Reed. "Where are you?" he asked when Reed finally answered.

"I can't make it tonight, sorry."

"What do you mean you can't make it?" he growled, then slipped the love note into his jacket pocket. He and Dylan were at the Blue Velvet Bar for their almost weekly get-together, and had been waiting for Reed, but the guy was now dropping out. Rourke knew that it was only a matter of time before these get-togethers stopped completely.

"Leave him alone," Dylan whispered, as he slid into the comfy booth. But he'd said it loud enough that Reed heard.

"Do what Dylan says," Reed suggested, "Leave me alone."

"Why don't you come on out anyway, and we can talk?" He sensed his friend was going through a lot right now, and he wanted to be there for him. Equally, having received a fourth notecard this morning, Rourke was desperate to tell his friends about the problems plaguing him.

"Next time. I've got too much going on the business front to bore the heck out of you both."

"Suit yourself," said Rourke. "You know where we are if you change your mind." He hung up.

"You shouldn't force him," Dylan told him. "He'll come out when he's good and ready."

"What if he's sinking into depression?"

"Reed's not going to sink into depression."

"How do you know?"

"I know."

Rourke rolled his eyes. "I suppose I should thank you for coming out tonight."

Dylan seemed to have picked up on his flippant tone. "What's that supposed to mean?"

Rourke sat back and placed his forearms on the table. "Well, it's only a matter of time before you get too busy to come out. I'm surprised you didn't ditch me tonight."

Dylan groaned in irritation. "You're annoyed about something. What is it? Work?"

"Work's keeping me busy." He wrestled with the thought of telling Dylan, and then wondered at the same time if it would be a good idea. Dylan was the softer of the two, and maybe it wasn't such a bad thing that Reed wasn't here. It might be wise to run his love notes saga by Dylan because having both of his friends present ran the risk of him being made fun of. And he wasn't feeling up to being the clown.

"And what else, apart from work?" Dylan asked, suspicious. Rourke lifted the beer bottle to his lips. "We hired the new guy."

"The one who was on his probationary period?"

He took a gulp, then placed the bottle on the table, nodding. "That's the one. He's good. And guess who came over from the agency to get the papers signed?"

Dylan shook his head and gave a half-shrug.

"Shay Donovan."

When Dylan blinked in ignorance, Rourke reminded him. "Jenna's friend. It was her and Jenna, and maybe a couple of others, who turned up to Reed's party back in high school."

"Did she recognize you?"

"She did. She's the one who said we went to school together, while I was still trying to figure out where I knew her from."

"I'm surprised she didn't give you the cold shoulder, knowing what you guys did to those poor girls."

"She told me not to worry about it, that school was a long time ago."

"You brought that up?" Dylan asked, surprised. It made him wonder what was wrong with that. "Yeah, so? I was trying to break the ice."

"By bringing up something that happened years ago?"

"I was trying to prompt her memory and tell her that I was a friend of Reed's, you know, given that our friend is going out with her friend."

"Why did that matter?"

"Look, pal," said Rourke, getting annoyed. "I was just trying to make conversation."

"Right." Dylan still looked at him as if he was crazy, which made Rourke wonder if he had been out of line starting that line of conversation. He'd been coming at it purely from an investigative angle, because—and it always came down to this—he viewed every woman who crossed his path as a possible sender of the love notes.

It could literally be anyone from Starling Bay. The envelopes were all postmarked from here. Having lived here all his life, he knew most of the women in the town, and he was pretty sure he'd checked out most of the good-looking ones in his age range. He knew of them, even if he didn't know them too well.

He had so far built up his short list—a loose, but on balance, fairly robust short list, which now consisted of Roxy, possibly Mackenzie, and perhaps…at lesser odds, Shay, and at even lesser odds, Daisy.

He hadn't given Daisy any particular thought, but this morning she had said in a particularly provocative tone, that his mail had come. And lo and behold, among the various letters had been the latest love note.

He'd dismissed Daisy because she was in her early twenties, he guessed, and she had only started last summer, and more because he didn't want it to be her. But something about the way she'd spoken to him this morning made him reconsider her as a possibility. And now, the more he thought about it, the more it was starting to make sense. She blushed each time he walked past the reception desk, and he noticed she was particularly clumsy when he was around. She'd dropped letters, dropped the newspaper, had managed to tip over a flowerpot and had knocked her glass of water over on more than one occasion.

He knew he had an effect on women, but it seemed to be more pronounced around Daisy. Either she was clumsy all the time, or she was especially clumsy when he was around.

The arrival of the latest note made him determined to seek out the woman behind them.

Dylan was texting again and this enraged Rourke further.

"Could you get off your phone, and talk to me at least? You're like a teen texting his new girlfriend."

"I feel like a teen texting my new girlfriend," joked Dylan, before making an apologetic face. "Sorry. Merry wasn't sure if I was eating out with you guys, or whether I was going to go to her place for dinner."

"What did you tell her?"

Dylan seemed to struggle to say something. "I told her that we might finish early tonight."

"Great." It was obvious that Dylan didn't have much time for him either. Now he felt hurt and angry.

"Hey, look. I didn't mean to offend you, but you seem miles away. I'm getting the impression you don't want to be here," said Dylan.

"Me?"

"Forget it," Dylan backtracked. "I'll call Merry and tell her to go ahead and eat without me. I didn't mean anything by it, I assumed it wasn't going to be a late night because Reed's not here."

"But *I'm* here. Don't you think I have anything to add to the conversation?" Too bad that he had something on his mind he needed to get out, and wasn't sure how to mention it.

"Sorry," Dylan replied. "You've been really grouchy tonight. Dyson coming down on you hard?"

"Dyson's going to have me working with him to sell one of those big old mansions near where Reed lives."

"In Glassmere? Houses around there don't go up for sale very often."

"They don't. They're passed down to heirs. Either way, the commission is going to be huge."

"A five-figure commission?"

"Hopefully." He was eager to give this his best shot. "Say," he cleared his throat, not sure how to start off on this. "What if…"

"What if what?"

"What if…" He shifted in his seat before picking up his bottle of beer again. "Someone…"

"If someone what, Rourke?"

Just as he'd been about to tell him, he now held back, not sure if he should tell Dylan.

"Hey!" Roxy waved at them as she and her groups of friends walked past them and headed towards the exit. "Hey," they nodded in unison.

Roxy had been here the entire time? She and her friends must have been sitting towards the back because he hadn't seen her until now.

"What's she doing out?" he asked Dylan.

"Out?" Dylan laughed. "She's not caged."

"But I've never seen her here before," Rourke said.

Dylan snorted. "Of course she's been here before. What a crazy thing to say."

"Out of all the times we've been here, have you ever seen her?" This had to be a sign. It had to be.

"Are you feeling ill?" Dylan looked at him oddly. "Listen to yourself. Of course she's been here. I've seen her here a couple of times before."

"Not here. Not in this place, not when we've been here."

Dylan's eyes opened wide and he stared at him. "I need to get Reed over. What's the matter with you? You're not making sense. April Fool's day is coming up in a few days' time, but you're peaking a little too early. You're starting to worry me."

Rourke stared at Roxy and her group of friends as they left the bar. She looked pretty fine, he thought, in a sexy, short black dress, with knee-high boots, and a leather jacket. "She looks like a biker," he muttered, as if he wasn't entirely pleased with her ensemble. She looked hot. Sexy hot. That jacket would have done it for him once, but he could also see Roxy in something a little more classy.

Maybe he was just getting old.

Had she dressed up and intended to be here at a time when she'd known he would be here with his friends? It was entirely possible that he'd mentioned to her in passing that he and the boys met here around this time once a week.

This had to be more than a mere coincidence.

Maybe Roxy was the one?

"What were you going to tell me?" Dylan asked.

"Nothing." He couldn't see how he was going to explain it to Dylan in a way that wouldn't have his friend keel over in laughter at him. And, for now, he had another lead.

Roxy.

as there any point in continuing with these?

She wondered what he thought of them, whether it got him thinking about who the sender might be.

Was he curious to know?

She longed to know.

But was she willing to reveal herself? Was she ready to tell?

Would she ever tell?

Or would she let it die down so that she would never have to reveal her identity?

The question was, would Rourke be smart enough to figure it out for himself? Would he pass her 'depth' test?

What was she doing? Some days she considered it a ridiculous and childish folly.

Who in their right mind, at her age, and in this age of digital communication, would send out handwritten love poems?

It was glitter, she told herself. A tiny touch of sparkle in her life; excitement for her, and hopefully something to liven up his day.

CHAPTER 8

His own office. Rourke huffed out a satisfied breath, looking at his huge wooden desk, and his own four walls. And no colleague to have to share it with. His own office again.

Phil was moving into the office he was vacating but Angelo had opted to take over Rourke's old desk. He'd emptied his drawers earlier and moved all of his files and belongings over to his new office as Angelo slowly moved over.

"All settled in?" Angelo asked, hovering near the door.

"Yeah. You?"

"All done," Angelo replied, walking in.

"Phil didn't mind that you hogged my desk?"

"Nah. He let me have it."

"You'll like my desk, and my chair," said Rourke, sitting back in his plush executive leather chair.

"You don't look as if you miss it," Angelo remarked.

"I don't."

"You look pretty comfortable here." Angelo walked towards him and handed him a note. "I found this. It must have fallen through the cracks in the drawer."

It was a love note. Rourke stared at it for a split second, his mind going haywire, wondering if Angelo had read it. "Thanks," he said, taking it and throwing it into his new drawer. Damn those pesky little things. He should have just ripped them all to shreds.

"Sorry, I couldn't help but read it."

"You read it?" Embarrassment heated his face.

"I didn't know whose it was." Angelo folded his arms.

"You moved to my desk, pal. Whose did you think it was?" The words came out harsher than he'd intended. "It's nothing. Just a… a little note."

"It's a cute poem. Who wrote it, your niece or something?"

Rourke cringed at the insult. Not that he had a niece, but likening this to something written by a child?

"Something like that." He forced a smile as Angelo walked away, leaving him to consider the possibility that the whole thing might have been one big prank. Maybe he was taking these notes too seriously.

He opened up the notecard—the first one he'd received on Valentine's Day—and glanced at the lines again:

Lost, not to be found,
Liked, never to be loved,
Light, yet still heavy,
Heavy, my heart, drowns.

Angelo was wrong. This couldn't have been written by a kid, or even a teen, or someone just wanting to prank him, surely?

But what if someone was having a joke at his expense? Maybe it was time to take it as if it were a joke, as if the sender wasn't being serious and was only doing this out of a distorted sense of fun? It was slightly macabre, thinking of it that way, but it might be better for his sanity.

Deciding that he needed his afternoon sugar rush, he headed towards Books & Buns again.

He walked into the bookshop feeling happier than when he'd left the office. Angelo's patronizing remark forgotten, he strode up to the counter, had a look around, couldn't find any lemon drizzle loaves or slices, or cinnamon buns, and no sign of Leigh either.

One of the part-time assistants was at the service counter, so he ordered an ordinary blueberry muffin and a cup of coffee, and sat at one of the tables. He got out the paperwork he'd brought with him, and started to look through the notes on the mansion in Glassmere.

"Hey." Leigh walked past him with a tray in her hands. "You came too late."

"For what?"

"I made low-fat cookies and muffins this morning. They're all gone."

He blinked. "How many did you make?"

"A whole tray's worth. They sold like hotcakes! I wish I'd saved you some."

"Not a problem that you didn't," he replied, somewhat relieved. The whole point of cakes and cookies was that they tasted good, because they were rich, and sweet and yummy. Low-fat, and reduced-sugar, and flourless, and all those other bland-sounding things didn't belong with cakes and cookies. But what did he know?

"I'll put some aside for you next time," said Leigh, clearing away the cups and plates from the empty tables. She was obviously eager for him to try her new recipes.

"That's not really necessary."

"I only made them because you suggested it."

"I didn't suggest anything of the sort!"

"You're watching your weight," she reminded him.

That was true. Not that he was strictly keeping to his diet. It was still sweet of her, though. He watched as she filled up her tray. "Got a moment?"

"Sure, what is it?" She set the tray back down again and moved closer.

"Sit down for a moment." And when she did, "You remember that day you picked up that note?"

Her brow quirked. "What note?"

Out of his back slacks pocket, he pulled the note Angelo had found. "Similar to this one." He kept it closed, and showed her the front face of it. It was different than the one she'd picked up the other day, but they were all similar-ish.

"Oh, I remember," she said slowly.

His eyes moved right then left, as if he was watching for secret agents who might have infiltrated the bookshop. "Someone," he whispered, his voice low, and husky, "Someone has been sending me them."

Leigh double-blinked. "Sending them?"

"Through the mail. Straight to my work address."

She shook her head. "I don't follow."

What was so hard to follow? "Someone—I don't know who—has been mailing these…these…love notes to me. I've had four so far. Look," he opened it up and showed her the poem. It was the second one he'd received. She stared at the handwriting:

Every once in a while you will meet
Someone who sweeps you off your feet
But what if that someone is unaware
What then, my friend, do I do this, do I dare?

"That's so sweet! 'Someone who sweeps you off your feet'. It's *so* romantic, Rourke," she gushed, then looked at his perplexed face. He wasn't smiling. "You don't think so?"

"I don't know what to think of it," he grumbled.

"But it must be exciting, not knowing who it's from, but knowing you have a secret admirer out there?"

"Trust me, it is for a while, but when you don't know who it could be…"

"Don't you have *any* idea?"

"Nope."

"An ex-girlfriend?"

He made a face. "I haven't had a girlfriend for a while now. You know that. And how far back would I go? Like, why would someone from my past want to send me these now?"

"You must have *some* idea?" she said, sitting forward and taking a look at the note again. "This is so cute!" she squealed.

He huffed out an irritated breath.

"You really have *no* idea?" Leigh asked.

"None."

"Not even a clue?" Leigh persisted. "What about the people you work with? Could it be anyone there?"

"No." He no longer counted Daisy as a strong contender. After careful consideration, he'd taken her off his short list, so he didn't even bother to mention her. "I did wonder if it might be…" He paused.

"Who?"

"Someone I used to go to school with a long time ago."

"Like who?"

"Shay Donovan…maybe. I don't even know why I'm telling you this, but it feels like a huge relief."

"Why do you think it's her?"

"I don't. I have a hunch it might be her. Or Roxy, we had a couple of dates years ago." He drummed his fingers on the table then whispered, "or maybe the florist."

"Mackenzie?"

"You know her?"

"We live in the same apartment building, we're both small shop owners, of course I know her."

He grew cautious, preferring not to give too much away.

"Why do you think it's her?"

"Just a hunch."

Leigh looked over his shoulder. "Uh-oh, it's getting busy again. I have to go." She got up and picked up the tray from the next table. "Good luck with your search."

"Thanks."

"If you come by in the next few days I'll have some more low-calorie muffins for you to try."

"You don't need to count the calories," he exclaimed.

"I meant for you." She laughed. "Hope you find the mystery lady, Poirot."

He sat back, picked up his coffee cup, and wished the same.

CHAPTER 9

They were in Roxy's Diner having lunch. For Rourke, this doubled as an investigative move, as well as getting him out of the office.

"When Dyson tells you your pitch better be tight, it better be tight," he told Angelo.

"Got it." Angelo looked grim.

"Loosen up, pal. This is just a little pep talk, nothing more."

"Thanks, I appreciate it."

"And remember, the first rule of selling any property: find the lady of the house, if there is one. I'm not saying flirt with the ladies, I'm saying just show them the kitchen, the oven, the view from the kitchen sink, and get them to fall in love with those things, because women love their own space, and the kitchen is their domain. Get the wife or girlfriend to fall in love with the tiling, and the stove, and the oven, and you're halfway there. Because once you sell the idea that the kitchen is an amazing feature of the house, and you infer that they'd be crazy not to want it, you're that much closer to a sale, and," he raised his hand and rubbed his fingers together, "a nice, big, fat commission check."

"Oh, puh-leeeese." Roxy set down two cans of orangeade, and two glasses. "That's the most asinine, patronizing, stereotypical garbage I've ever heard, and I've heard plenty in my line of work. Don't listen to him," she told Angelo.

Rourke lifted his head and crossed his arms in amusement. "There's a big difference between selling million-dollar properties and a plate of pasta, Rox."

"Oh, yeah?" Her hands flew to her hips and she turned all defensive. "If a salesman said that stuff to me, I'd throw something at him."

"You would not!"

"I'd walk away." She snapped her fingers like a diva and walked away. Angelo looked as if he was trying hard to maintain a serious expression. "I think you just got told, pal."

"Rox doesn't sell multi-million dollar houses, and if she had the chance to make five-figure commission checks, she would do whatever it took. I know what I'm talking about, trust me. What I'm telling you works on the wives and girlfriends, I swear." He was the top salesman at the office. Not for nothing did Dyson have him working on the Glassmere property. "I know how to win the women over, and let's face it, whether a couple buys a house or not, the decision will come down to the wife or girlfriend."

"No smart woman is going to fall for that nonsense," Roxy muttered, as she sailed past.

"I could sell you a house, Rox," said Rourke, excited by the challenge.

"Oh, yeah?" She stopped in her tracks, her hands flying to her waist again. She stared at him as if daring him. "Sell it to me, then. What would you say? Because all that lovemaking over the kitchen appliances isn't going to cut it, and believe me, I *know* my appliances."

Challenge accepted, Rourke sat up straighter, and stared into her eyes. "I'd have you feel the soft carpet under your feet when you get out of bed. I'd show you the view of the yard from the window. In the kitchen, I'd show you the light, and the airiness and the sheer size of the kitchen, and the shiny graphite worktops glistening under the lights. I'd show you the state-of-the-art appliances, and the large kitchen island with its sleek and shiny white countertop." He'd lowered his voice, and waited for her comeback, but there was none. She was speechless, and he knew he'd done well. "Isn't that right, Rox?" he asked softly.

"It might get you a second viewing," she said, and clicked on her heels and left.

Angelo laughed. "You sold it to her. I'm impressed. Phil said I'd learn a lot from you."

"It's a shame he didn't pick up much from me," replied Rourke. "It wasn't as if I didn't try."

Roxy came by again, and set down their plates. "Two salads, one with a jacket potato, and one... with nothing Are you still watching what you eat?" Roxy asked him.

He tapped his belly. "Got to keep in shape."

"You're just fishing for a compliment," she huffed, "Don't think I'm going to give you one."

"You were looking pretty hot when I saw you at the Blue Velvet a couple of weeks ago, Rox. See, I don't mind giving compliments where they're due. What were you doing there?"

"Same thing you were, most likely," she replied, not giving him an answer. "Don't forget," she said, pointing a finger at him, "You need to let me know about numbers for that party."

He almost groaned out loud. "I forgot," he said, completely forgetting his earlier plan.

"What party?" Angelo asked when Roxy left.

"Don't worry about it. It's not likely to go ahead."

That seemed to be enough for Angelo. "That Roxy chick, you know her?"

"Of course I know her. I know most of the women in this town. Why?"

"I think she likes you."

"Nah, that's how we always talk." Rourke looked over at Roxy. "We go back a long time."

"I'm telling you," Angelo insisted. "Did you read her body language?"

Rourke looked up, glanced over at Roxy to make sure she wasn't within earshot. "What body language?"

"The way she was looking at you, and standing with her hands on her hips, joking and chatting to you. She couldn't keep away."

"That's because she was serving us our food." His brain was already doing overtime trying to figure out the mystery of the love notes, but he'd pushed it to the back of his mind because he was so busy working on the Glassmere property.

"I reckon she likes you," Angelo insisted.

"I know her from school, and we dated a couple of times, but we didn't hit it off. Besides, we always talk like that. We're friends."

"Hmmm. Maybe you and her are too similar," Angelo remarked. Rourke lifted his head and eyed the pretty brunette. Rox had always been like that around him, maybe they were just too comfortable and familiar around each other to be anything else.

"What do you know of Shay?" he asked Angelo, now that his friend had him wondering about women suitors.

"Shay? You mean from the agency?"

Rourke snorted. "Yes, from the agency. How many Shays do you know?"

"Why do you want to know?"

Rourke considered the question. Could he trust Angelo, if he told him about the notes? He wiped his mouth with a napkin.

"You remember that note you gave back to me? You found it when you moved to my desk?"

"The one your niece wrote?"

Rourke let out an exasperated groan. "I don't have a niece. I have a secret admirer, though. At least, I think I do."

"A what?"

"You heard, don't make me say it again."

Angelo put down his knife and fork in surprise. "I wish I had one of those. How do you know?"

"Because she's sending me these love notes."

Angelo's eyebrow lifted. "Someone is sending you those, and you have no idea?"

"None, whatsoever."

"Just the one?"

"Four so far."

Angelo's head snapped back. "Dude," he said, flashing him a congratulatory smile. "That is some accomplishment."

Rourke's face sobered. "Selling a million dollar property is an accomplishment, pal. Not this. Haven't you paid attention to anything I've taught you?"

Angelo picked up his cutlery again. "Can we not talk work for a while. This is more exciting. You have a lady friend, and you don't know who. That's why you're asking about Shay?"

"She's a friend of a friend," Rourke told him, but Angelo was already shaking his head.

"Dude, it's not going to be a friend of a friend."

"But I know her, sort of," he insisted. "She was in my grade at school."

Angelo didn't look convinced. "It's not going to be someone like that, unless it's a psycho who barely knows you and that's not the type of attraction you'd want."

Rourke listened and considered this sage advice. "Daisy, the receptionist," he offered, on a whim.

"Daisy?" The way Angelo said it, made Rourke think that Angelo liked her. She was young and unburdened, like Angelo. The kind of girl who came to work because she needed to, the kind who was happy with her nine to five on weekdays. The type of girl who was content with her month-end paycheck, and had no major expectations from her life. It seemed too simple, too easy for someone like her to resort to sending those notes. Plus, aside from her general clumsiness, and his aversion to dating colleagues, he hadn't felt any spark around her.

"Who else could it be, that you sort of know, to talk to?"

Angelo's sudden interest got him thinking out loud. "There's the florist, Mackenzie."

"Aw, yeah," said Angelo, nodding with a smile on his face. Rourke looked at him in disbelief. "You know her too?"

"No," Angelo replied, "but she's hard to miss, especially with those curls and those long, long legs. She's a beauty, and she's also totally wasted behind the shop counter. She could easily be a model."

Rourke blinked at Angelo. This guy was scarily like him. The similarities were uncanny and beginning to freak him out. But Angelo had a point. He himself had once considered that it might be Mackenzie, and he was starting to see that Angelo might be right; that perhaps Roxy wasn't a contender.

CHAPTER 10

*H*e had lots of late nights at work, lots of time spent in meetings with Tony, and it all helped him to focus. But even so, at the back of his mind, he knew that the next notecard—if indeed, there was going to be another one—would be here in a couple of days' time.

He passed by the florist's shop one afternoon on his way to the bookshop again, but just as he walked past and peeked through the open door, a row of silver buckets ablaze with colorful bunches of flowers caught his attention. Drawn to them, he went inside and saw Mackenzie talking to a customer. He made himself busy looking at the flower displays.

"Hey there." Her soft voice behind him made him turn around. "Sorry to keep you waiting." She wore her hair pulled back in a thick ponytail today, and revealed her face, her features sharp, her cheekbones high. Angelo was right. She was a stunner.

"That's okay. I was walking past and I got sucked in by your flower displays again. They're always so eye-catching."

"They're meant to be, and thank you for the compliment."

"They just literally caught my eye. Hard to not come inside."

"Then my magic is working." She smiled the kind of smile

that would have had him buying her a drink, if they were in the bar right now. "Are you looking for anything in particular?"

He was so taken in by her smile, by her voice, by her appearance—the whole perfect package, that he forgot about the flowers.

"Uh..." he sighed, not wanting to leave just yet. "I haven't made my mind up yet. What do you recommend?"

"It depends on who they're for. A girlfriend, a friend, your mother...a work colleague?"

"Hmm." He didn't have anyone he wanted to buy flowers for. "I'll just take a look and see what catches my fancy," he said, rather than answering her question.

"Take your time. I'll be over by the table."

He hovered around, admiring the baskets full of different cut flowers, and the made-up bouquets. He hadn't intended to buy anything when he had walked in but he couldn't leave empty-handed, especially since he'd made such a big show about it. He reached for a bunch of colorful tulips and took them over to her.

"That's a lovely choice," she commented, taking the bunch and wrapping it up in her signature black and pink paper.

"They're colorful. They'll brighten up the place." Whose place, he wasn't sure of. "Bloom," he commented, snatching at the chance to make conversation. "That's a good choice of a name."

She looked at him as if she couldn't figure out if he was being serious or joking. "Thanks. My mom suggested Blossom."

"Blossom," he repeated. "That's not bad either. I like Bloom. It's more memorable, short and classy."

"It's from my grandmother, actually," she said, volunteering extra information and giving him the chance to admire her gorgeous face. How come he had never before noticed just how pretty she was? "Your grandmother?"

"She always used to say to me, 'be like the one and only Mackenzie'."

He repeated the phrase in his mind, trying to connect the dots, then, "Be like the one and only Mackenzie?" he said out loud.

"B-L-O-O-M," Mackenzie spelled the letters out for him.

The penny dropped. He laughed, and then the laugh stuck in his throat, and he stopped.

"Of course it doesn't really make sense," she said quickly, using her hand to gesticulate. But he hadn't stopped because it didn't make sense. It made perfect sense to him. "It's clever," he said, rushing to reassure her. BLOOM was perfect. Some dots connected in his brain for him to take away and analyze the bigger picture later.

"My grandma had a lot to do with my upbringing and she always used to say that to me. It was like a mantra," Mackenzie continued, giving him a window into her life. "And it helped especially when the girls at school teased me."

"They teased you?" he asked, shocked to hear this. He couldn't see what anyone would want to tease her about, this vision of loveliness before him.

"I was tall and gangly, and in my teens I towered over most of the girls, and some of the boys. And I had freckles, and a bushy mane of hair."

He stared back in silent surprise. "They were jealous."

"I'm not sure it was jealousy. They were just plain nasty. Girls can be."

He hadn't been expecting the conversation to turn heavy so quickly. "I'm sorry to hear that." He didn't know what else to say. "They were obviously wrong, and silly, and I still maintain it's because they were jealous. I think your freckles are cute."

She averted her gaze as if she was embarrassed. "Thanks."

He stared at her, knowing that the things she had been bullied for in her youth were the very things that probably made people turn their heads each time she walked past. "Tall and gangly you might have been, but modelesque, I think, is the right word."

"My grandma always used to say that, when she'd catch me in tears," she looked away, a wistful smile on her face as she recalled the memories, "She used to say those words to me … be like the one and only Mackenzie. I thought it was fitting to name this shop and to honor her wisdom."

He was so caught up in her story that he forgot to speak. Then he said, "You're stunning, and don't let anyone else tell you otherwise." He meant it, too. She smiled, and looked obviously embarrassed by his sudden outburst of compliments. He bade her goodbye and left, walking down the street with his heart thumping as if he'd just asked a girl out for the very first time.

BLOOM

What a story.

And she'd told it to him—a person she barely knew. Maybe because he was a person she wanted to get to know better.

The idea wasn't completely ludicrous.

It *could* be her. There was a strong possibility that it was her. They'd just had a real proper conversation, and one in which she had opened up to him. She'd told him about her school days, and her bullying and her grandma; personal things.

They had gone from being relative strangers to *this*. And, to cement it all, the name of her shop, and the way it had come about; it was Mackenzie.

It had to be.

Angelo had been right.

He walked into Books & Buns and looked around for Leigh. She was opening up boxes of books over by one of the display tables, and smiled at him as he walked towards her.

"Lovely flowers." She nodded at the wrapped up bunch in his hands. He pointed them at her, the pink and white tulip heads just peeping out at the top. "They're yours."

She blushed in surprise, and she didn't seem to know what to say.

"Seriously, they're yours." He waited for her to take them. "I walked past Bloom, and these caught my eye. For you."

Her lips formed into an 'O' shape, then closed. She blinked. "Well, thank you, but why are you giving me flowers?"

"Oh, long story, but I had to buy them. Come on over, and I'll tell you."

"Don't you want to order any food, first?" She followed him to an empty table.

"Not yet. I've figured out who it is," he said, sitting down.

For a moment she looked confused. "Who what is?"

"I've figured out who sent the notes."

Her eyes snapped wide open with curiosity. "Your secret love note sender?"

"Yes."

"Who?" Leigh set the flowers on the table, then sat down.

"The florist at Bloom."

A gasp of air escaped Leigh's mouth. "Mackenzie?"

"Yes."

"What makes you think it's her?"

He repeated the conversation he'd had with Mackenzie.

"She told you she was bullied at school," said Leigh, "And how she came to name her shop, but I don't see how that means anything."

"We spoke. She confided in me, and she doesn't really know me, not like that."

"Like what?"

"Like enough to share that kind of a story with." The more he thought about it, the more he was convinced with his assessment. "You know her, don't you?" he asked, suddenly remembering.

"I know her. Why?" she asked, looking at him. "Do you want me to put in a good word for you?"

He laughed off her suggestion. "I don't need anyone to do that for me. I hadn't realized before how stunning she is. She's absolutely beautiful."

"She is," replied Leigh, agreeing. "And she's a beautiful person inside as well. That's a rare thing these days."

"Be like the one and only Mackenzie." It's a cool story, don't you think? And it's a play on words, which is why I think it's her."

"Why?"

"Because she has a thing about words, and therefore it's possible that she wrote those poems."

"I see the connection, but it's a very weak connection, Rourke."

"It's not weak," he exclaimed.

"I see that you want it to be her," Leigh observed. He couldn't agree more. "You're right. Out of everyone I've considered it to be, having it be Mackenzie would be the best." He couldn't help but smile just thinking about it. "She's a looker and a half."

"And you do have a thing for pretty women."

"I'm not that shallow, am I?"

Leigh didn't comment.

"I'm not that shallow," he insisted. "Up until a few days ago Angelo and I narrowed it down to—"

"Who's Angelo?"

"A new employee at work."

"You told him?"

"He found one of the notes. He thought it was cute that my niece wrote something so sweet."

"But you don't have a—"

"Exactly, I think I'd know if I had a niece," he replied, grinning.

It reminded him that his sister would be coming over soon to see him. "Hope you like the flowers," he said, nodding at the bunch on the table.

"I do, very much. Thank you."

"I hope they'll brighten your day."

"Like Mackenzie did yours?" she asked.

"A girl like that is bound to brighten any man's day." He stared over at the cake counter, squinting to get a better look. "Got any of those lemon drizzle loaves?"

"Not today, but I'm glad you came because you can try some of those healthy oatmeal cookies."

CHAPTER 11

Just like that the love notes stopped. They'd been arriving every two weeks, regular as clockwork. He should have received one a few days ago but nothing had been mailed to him. He didn't know whether to be relieved or disappointed.

Walking into the Blue Velvet Bar he saw Reed and Dylan sitting at their usual table. He was looking forward to an evening with his friends, especially given the fact that Reed was putting in an appearance this time.

"Hey!" he cried, slapping Reed on the back as he gave him a half-hug. "I see that you've made the effort."

"Been busy," replied Reed. Rourke acknowledged Dylan as he sat down, then slapped Reed on the back. "Now you need to tell us what you've been up to."

"I've been getting on with my life. Sorting out stuff, you know, canceling wedding arrangements, talking to friends and family and trying to explain why the wedding didn't go ahead, gave an interview to the local paper—"

"Yeah, I saw that," Rourke exclaimed.

"I was surprised," added Dylan, "Given that you hate talking about your private life, and you hate giving interviews."

"Had to do it. Couldn't sit back and let Olivia get away with her lies."

"What's she doing now?" Rourke asked, out of curiosity.

"Why, are you interested?" Reed shot back.

"Heck, no."

"Are you sure? Because you seemed pretty interested in Jenna last time as well."

"I was being polite, making her feel at home." That night at the Valentine's Day ball, when Jenna had been working at the Reed mansion, Rourke knew he'd been overly chatty to her, but he'd had his reasons. "I didn't know back then, about you and her."

"There was no me and her at that time, not really. Not properly." Reed clarified.

"Oh?" Dylan asked, sitting up straighter. "And now?"

Rourke's ears also pricked up at this news and they both waited for Reed to elaborate.

"Now, it's different." Reed raised his hand to catch the attention of a server.

"Yeah?" Rourke asked.

"What's changed?" Dylan chimed in.

"We started work on the old movie theater," said Reed, annoyingly deflecting the topic.

Rourke called a server and they all placed their drinks orders while Reed talked about his latest project.

"And what else has changed?" he asked, when Reed was done. News of the old movie theater was interesting, but it wasn't the news they wanted.

"Me and Jenna." Reed stared at them, his eyes glittering.

"You and Jenna what?" Rourke asked.

"Are you going to continue with your fascination over my

girlfriend?" Reed asked him. He smiled at that. The grin spreading from ear to ear.

"Girlfriend?" So Reed and Jenna were finally together?

"I knew it was just a matter of time," exclaimed Dylan, as the server set down their drinks.

"Had to take it slow," said Reed, looking at the table, lost in his own little world. A smile played across his features, and for a moment it seemed as if he'd locked them out of whatever it was he was thinking about.

"That's probably a good thing," Rourke commented. Reed had been through enough ups and downs ever since last summer when he'd told them about his quick-as-lightning engagement to Olivia Sykes. He and Dylan had both been guarded and wary about it ever since, because that wasn't what Reed was like. He never did things on the spur of the moment.

So when Reed had announced that the engagement had broken off, it had come as a surprise at first, but then it made sense. Reed hadn't exactly looked like a picture of happiness in the past few months. But right now, the guy looked like he was beaming.

"Slow, on account of many things. But, you could say, we're together now."

"Yeah?"

"We're dating."

Dylan raised his beer bottle. "Awesome." They clinked their drinks. "At least we've met Jenna," Rourke said dryly, noting how different things had been the last time, when Reed had returned from his long business trip to Manhattan with a fiancée. "And he's known Jenna since schooldays."

"I like her," Dylan replied.

"Me too." He and Dylan were doing this on purpose, talking about Jenna and excluding Reed from the conversation.

"She's good for me," Reed replied, watching them both with amusement.

"She's different from Olivia," Rourke commented, and at the same time wondered how Reed's parents were with the whole situation now. From what Reed had told them last time, his father particularly hadn't been so enamored about the break-up with Olivia. And from what he knew of Reed's dad, he wondered how he might take to the news of Reed with someone who used to be his maid.

"It sure is good to see you again," he said, pleased to see his friend back to normal again, and pleased that the three of them were meeting up again.

"What's your news?" Reed asked Dylan.

"Merry bought one of the one-story houses in Forest Heights. She left her job in Boston last month, and she's moving here around Easter time. I'm going to drive to Boston to help her move out."

"Then we can expect a wedding in Starling Bay, after all?" Rourke asked. At this rate his friends would be settled with children in no time, and he'd be left wondering what the heck had happened.

Would he ever get to find out the identity of the person behind the love notes? Now that they had stopped, he felt as if something was missing. There had been a glimmer of anticipation and he would wonder when he'd get the next one. He was none the wiser now but he felt far more detached from it all. Truth was, he was starting to get fed-up. He'd been caught up in the idea of it being Mackenzie but now he wasn't so sure.

Any which way he looked at it, the whole thing was an unwanted distraction, and one he didn't need.

"No wedding, yet, or engagement, or anything else," Dylan replied. "Like Reed, we're taking things slow. There's no rush. Merry's happy, and she has a lot of adjusting to do, plus Chloe starts school after Easter, so that will take time, and I've got a new baby elephant for a pet."

Rourke had heard about the dog, the Great Dane who had charged into Dylan's store and brought Merry and Dylan together.

"I bet he eats you out of house and home," Reed commented. "I've seen the size of that thing."

"He's a great dog," Dylan replied, defensively.

"Yeah, huge," replied Reed.

"I meant great as in amazing," said Dylan, shaking his head. "You've been very quiet," he said, turning to Rourke. Trust Dylan to have picked up on something. Rourke flinched inwardly. So far he hadn't mentioned anything about the love notes, and he wasn't sure he was even going to bring that up.

"Nothing going on with me," he replied, shaking his head before taking a long sip of his drink.

"How's the new recruit coming along?"

"You mean Angelo? He's doing good. He's moved into my old office and I've finally got an office to myself."

"Finally," said Reed. "I'd say we've got good news all around." They all raised their glasses again.

"Go a whole month without catching up and see how much progress we've made," said Dylan.

Rourke wondered whether to tell them about his secret admirer.

"I was waiting for your hundred and one questions about Jenna," said Reed, and then he laughed as if he'd made a funny joke.

"Hey, just to be clear, I wasn't after your girlfriend," Rourke insisted.

"Coulda fooled me," replied Reed, though he didn't seem perturbed by it.

"Yeah, we know what you're like."

That final comment from Dylan just about did him in. He

didn't deliberately court his reputation as a charmer, but he couldn't help it if women liked him. It wasn't his fault he was so popular, or had a way about him that women found appealing. "What am I like?" he asked, curious now to know exactly what his friends thought of him. It had been a perennial joke among them all for years, that Reed was the more astute and financially savvy of them, and that Dylan was the artsy, laidback guy, while he had been relegated to being the playboy. Now that he'd called them out on it, the question seemed to have left his friends baffled.

"What's brought this on?" Reed asked.

"Are you feeling okay?" Dylan's face filled with concern. But knowing his friends, he wasn't sure if their concern was genuine or whether they were going to start laughing any moment now.

"No, I want to know. You're always laughing about it, so tell me. What am I like?"

"A playboy, a tease, a charmer," Reed said.

"What's the matter?" Dylan asked, always the diplomat. "Turning thirty really has affected you. You don't want to talk about it, you don't want to celebrate it. You don't want to do anything and now you're asking us what we think of you. This isn't the Rourke we know and love."

How could he make these guys see that he had a lot of stuff going on, and all he'd wanted from tonight was just a relaxed evening with a few beers?

Reed moved his beer bottle away from his lips and eyed him carefully. "This is a first," he said, carefully setting the bottle down. He leaned towards him. Looked him in one eye then the other. "We had no idea you were finding it so tough."

"I'm not finding it tough," he cried. "It wasn't the right time for a celebration. Seriously, guys, it's no big deal. And you," he looked at Reed, "had so much going on what with the engagement breaking up and your parents being over, it seemed we all had stuff we were dealing with."

Silence hung over them, heavy with disbelief. They didn't seem to believe him, even though it was partly true. Maybe it was better to come out and tell them. The love notes weren't the reason he hadn't celebrated his birthday. He really didn't want a fuss, but everyone else was making a fuss that he wasn't making a fuss. He'd been distracted, and now he was going to tell them why.

"Well," he said, inhaling deeply. "If you really want to know…"

His friends leaned in, their eyes trained on his face as if he was about to recite the winning lottery numbers. "Yesssss," said Reed, slowly angling his head.

"I've …" It was hard to say. He glanced at his friends, saw the rapt attention on their faces. "I think I've got a secret admirer."

Reed looked confused, his brow crinkling into tiny furrows. Dylan squinted at him. "A secret admirer?"

"Yeah."

For the first time in a long time, his friends were speechless. Then Dylan asked, "Who?"

"I don't know, hence the 'secret'. The reason I asked so many questions about Jenna was because someone has been sending me notes and I thought it might be her."

"*Notes?*"

"As in bills?" Reed asked.

Rourke wiped the back of his neck with his hand. Heat rose inside him as he wondered what these two were thinking. "Sort of. Notes, really. Like cards. Like poems."

"Poems?" Dylan echoed.

"As in … roses are red, violets are blue?" Reed asked. Rourke grew suddenly suspicious.

"Like love letters?" Dylan asked.

"Not love letters," he growled.

"Not love letters but *poems?*" Reed asked.

"Since when?" Dylan wanted to know.

"Since Valentine's day."

"Valentine's Day?"

"Wasn't sure if it was a prank."

"What makes you think it's not a prank now?"

"You kept this quiet!" Dylan retorted.

"At first I thought it might be Jenna, because…well, what was I supposed to think? These notes started arriving a few weeks after I saw her in town, and …" he shrugged, "And then she started working for you. I had no real reason for thinking it might be her, just that we had history and here she was suddenly and then the notes started."

"That's why you were hounding her at the ball?" Reed asked.

"Did she say I hounded her?"

Reed declined to answer.

"But obviously it's not her," he continued.

"Obviously," replied Reed, his eyes narrowed. "What do they say?"

"Can we see a note?" Dylan asked, there was a look of amusement in his eyes.

"Yeah," said Reed, sounding eager. "Let's take a look at these love letters, I haven't had a girl give me those since I left preschool." His friends chortled at that, making him wish he hadn't bothered telling them. Dylan grew suddenly serious when Rourke didn't reply. "Let's see, we should be able to tell by the handwriting."

"Steady, guys." A million questions. He should have known. "I don't have them on me." He didn't carry them around like they were important or anything. They were in his briefcase, and even if he had them on him, he wouldn't show his friends. While they looked all attentive and interested, he couldn't put it past them to tease him about this mercilessly until his dying days.

"Just give us a taste then, of what's inside them," Dylan begged.

"I told you, I don't have any on me."

"How many have you received?" Reed asked.

"Four."

"Four?" they cried in unison.

"Since Valentine's Day."

"And you never said a word in all that time," cried Dylan.

"I've been busy."

"Give us a line that you remember," Dylan asked. He recited them a line that he remembered.

"Who do you think it could be?" Dylan asked.

"Could be anyone," Reed interjected, before he could answer. "He's dated half the women in Starling Bay."

Rourke ground out an exasperated sigh. "Who do you think it could be?" Dylan asked him again. Rourke wasn't sure he wanted to let them in on his ever-dwindling list of possibilities, but Leigh hadn't been able to shed a light on things, and Angelo didn't seem to know any better. Maybe Reed and Dylan could help. He told them of the possible senders.

"Shay? You mean Jenna's friend?" Reed asked.

"We know her," Rourke insisted. "And we have links to the agency she works for. We got Angelo through it, and she came to the office a few weeks ago."

"Just because you knew someone at school doesn't make them a suspect," Dylan pointed out.

"Suspect." Reed laughed so hard he had tears in his eyes, then Dylan joined in. Rourke felt even more isolated and annoyed, and waited for them to finish.

"Sorry," said Dylan, when they had calmed down.

"Sorry, pal," Reed said, his face turning suddenly serious.

"But I don't think it's her anymore. I think it might be someone else."

"Who?"

"The florist at Bloom," he told them, just to shut them up.

"Is that the tall girl with the curly hair?" Reed asked.

"You know her?"

"She came to the house with a truckload of flowers for that darned magazine photo shoot that Olivia insisted on having. Why do you think it's her?"

Rourke recounted his conversation with Mackenzie and then tried to think if she might have been around on the day he visited Reed's mansion, around the time of the photo shoot. But he couldn't remember.

Rourke and Dylan looked at one another and shook their heads. "It can't be her," said Dylan, finally. "You two barely know one another. Just because she opened up and told you about her being bullied at school doesn't mean anything. I don't think a woman you barely know is going to send you poems. Women just aren't made like that."

"Spoken like a man who understands women," added Reed. "I second that theory. I don't think it's the florist either."

Rourke slumped back in his seat. He was fast losing the will to find out, and a part of him wished he hadn't told the guys. "It looks like they've stopped, so I'm just going to forget they ever happened." He picked up the food menu. "I'm hungry. Do either of you want to get a quick bite to eat or will you get whipped by your girlfriends if you don't go back and eat with them?"

Both his friends hesitated before replying, and when they agreed to get something to eat here, he hoped they weren't doing it out of pity.

CHAPTER 12

How hard it beats, my heart with fear,
that you will not hold any of this dear,
Or should I be brave, and fearless and smart,
And be the one to lay claim to your heart?

*S*he stared at the poem and wondered if she should send it. A man like Rourke, so confident, so charming, so comfortable around women, a man like that would never notice her.

Who was she, but a nobody?

She didn't want to think about the embarrassment at being found out. It would be insurmountable.

She slipped the notecard into the envelope and stared at it for the longest time.

CHAPTER 13

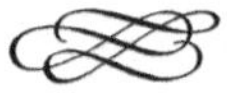

"You still haven't gotten back to me about your party."

He looked at Roxy, confused.

"Your thirtieth birthday party, remember, for ten to thirty people?"

He blinked. "I changed my mind."

"Why?"

"Too busy."

"Too busy to have a party? Rourke, you've changed!"

He was hovering over by the deli counter, trying to decide what he wanted to have for lunch, but now he found his appetite had disappeared. He had never intended to have a party, but he couldn't tell Roxy that. The conversation with his friends last week had left him even more fed up and annoyed about his secret admirer. He was just grateful that the notes had stopped, and didn't care anymore that he wasn't any closer to finding out who it was, and he'd forget about it all were it not for Angelo's continued questioning. He wished the guy would just shut up about it.

"It was just an idea," he replied, deciding that he didn't want anything. Not even a bottle of pop. He didn't even need a sample of her handwriting anymore because it didn't matter. None of this mattered.

"Are you okay?" Roxy asked, concerned enough that she'd walked over to his side, leaving the deli counter to her assistant.

"Yeah, why?"

"You seem down, and you're usually a bundle of laughs."

"I'm busy at work," he replied defensively. "Got one of those expensive properties over in Glassmere to sell."

"Someone's in for a huge bonus once that deal is made." She poked him gently in the shoulder, "You're doing well these days."

"Yeah? Thanks." He wondered what she meant by 'you're doing well these days.' Could it be that she was starting to see him in a different way? Maybe even as a potential suitor now that they were probably both in their thirties, and their circle of friends and acquaintances were starting to get married. Roxy, like Reed, seemed obsessed by her business. She was always at the diner, and if not at the front of the shop, then behind the scenes, overseeing the kitchen, pitching in and helping out whenever they fell short.

"Do you remember that time we double-dated?"

Her brow furrowed, and she smiled. "Why are you remembering that?"

"No reason," he replied quickly, and saw that this was his chance to find out. "That was strange, wasn't it?"

"You and me?" She made a face. "Yeah…it's strange thinking about it now."

"I know, right?" He laughed out extra loud, and at the same time tried to figure out if she was putting this on, or if it might be a hint of a clue.

But then, Roxy wasn't that type of woman. If she liked him, she would have told him to his face, just the way she'd stopped all chances of a second date from that double-date by telling him that they weren't going to work out.

"What can I get you?" she asked.

"Uh… I'll just take a salad," he replied, "Just a small one." He wasn't hungry, but, he would feel silly leaving without buying anything.

"A small salad," said Roxy, raising an eyebrow. "You're being really good with your diet."

He smiled, and patted his stomach. "It seems to be helping."

He left Roxy's Diner and headed back to work, contemplating things along the way. Now that the notes had stopped, and he wasn't wasting his time wondering who the culprit was, he felt a lot calmer.

He had gotten all carried away before because each time he spoke to someone, he went away thinking it could be her. These love notes had skewed his thought process and messed with his brain. No more. He had the Glassmere property to work on, and he wanted that big fat commission check. That had to be his primary focus.

"Hey," Angelo drawled the moment Rourke was about to sit down at his desk to eat his salad.

"What?" Rourke asked, seeing that the guy was still hovering by the door. Angelo looked left and right and then came in, closing the door behind him. "Ever consider that it might be Daisy?"

Oh, lord, no. "Ugh," he ground out, annoyance creeping over him. "No." Never Daisy.

"Think about it," urged Angelo, his eyes glittering with excitement.

"I'm at the stage now where I don't care about who it is, or was."

"But I saw some notes over by her desk, they're different than your one, but they're pretty, and white, and …got some birds on them."

"Drop it, Angelo. I'm not interested."

"Not even if it's Daisy?"

"Especially if it's Daisy." That would cause more problems than not. And nobody in their right mind would want an admirer from work. If it was someone at work, he'd be feeling extra creeped out.

"Dude, she's gorgeous."

Rourke placed his fork down and wished Angelo would leave him in peace. "You like her?" he asked.

"Nah," Angelo backtracked quickly. "I was just saying. You might want to go and check out those notecards."

"Most women have notecards," he replied. "I don't care anymore. I don't want to know, and truth is, I haven't received another card and I think that's the end of it."

"You haven't"

"No. They just stopped, and I'm glad they did." In fact, when he got home tonight, he was going to burn them and pretend this whole sorry episode never happened.

"Anything else?" he asked, seeing that Angelo didn't look as if he was in a hurry to leave. "You're supposed to be going through some sales techniques with me, Dyson said you would."

"Sales techniques," he said, stifling his irritation. "Pull up a chair so that you can see my screen."

"But you're eating."

"I was eating when you came in," he complained. "Don't worry. I can multitask."

He went through the slides from the presentation he'd given to the sales team last month, and then answered all of Angelo's questions. By the time he'd finished eating, and finished with Angelo, he felt as if he'd had an intense work session, and he longed for his afternoon shot of caffeine.

He walked past the receptionist's desk and told her that he was going out for half an hour.

"Cake break?" she asked, smiling.

"You know my movements so well," he joked, then stopped for a brief second by her desk. Glancing down, he saw the notecards lying face up. But they were a pack of *Thank You* cards.

Nope, these weren't those cards, and Daisy wasn't the sender.

Before he knew it, he was back at Books & Buns. The bookshop had become his little respite. His haven. A place to mellow out in, read the paper, look over some books, listen to the quiet background chatter of people talking quietly. Leigh wasn't around, so he bought an orange blossom muffin, seeing that there was no sign of his most sought-after cakes. He ordered a shot of his favorite coffee, and sat away from the counter, preferring to eat in peace, and not be hassled by anyone at the office.

"Hey," he said when Leigh walked past carrying a couple of books. "Wondered where you were."

"We had another delivery of books," she explained, stopping by his table. "You're trying the orange blossom muffin?"

"I'm trying to up my daily fruit allowance."

She laughed. "That doesn't count. There's not even a real orange in there. Just a drop of essence."

"It must count for something." He took another bite. It wasn't bad. It was no lemon drizzle, but it wasn't bad.

"Back in a moment," she told him. "I'd better put these away before I ruin the pristine covers. Don't you just love the clean, fresh smell of new books?" She was gone before he could answer.

She hadn't stepped more than a few yards away when a man approached her with a book in his hands. "This isn't even written in English," he complained, speaking so loudly that Rourke heard every word. "I don't understand it."

Leigh's face registered surprise, a flicker of fear rushed across her eyes. Rourke sat up.

"Doctor Zhivago isn't to everyone's taste," Leigh replied calmly.

"But you recommended it. You like this rubbish. It doesn't even make sense." He was loud, and rude and the shop assistants and the people in the store looked up.

"It's not to everyone's taste." She was so calm, so polite.

"I want to buy it for my girlfriend. What do you suggest?"

"It depends on what your girlfriend likes."

He tried to catch Leigh's attention, but she wasn't looking at anyone except the nasty customer in front of her. Rourke was tempted to wade in and rescue her, but Leigh glanced at him quickly and gave a sight shake of her head.

He stopped then saw the man lean in and say something to Leigh close up. Then he turned around and walked away.

Rourke watched him all the way to the door, and when the man left, he walked up to Leigh. "What was all that about?"

"It was nothing. He was just a rude man being rude. We get the occasional customer like that. Not all of them are as nice as you."

"But that was unwarranted."

She shrugged.

"Are you okay?" he asked, seeing that her face was red.

"I'm okay."

"Are you sure? I wanted to come over and tell him to get lost."

"You can't say that."

"He can't say that to you."

"Some people are rude, you have to let it go."

He was amazed by the ease with which she was willing to let it go. He couldn't stand it when Angelo got a little cocky sometimes, but that was nothing compared to this. She looked beat, and tired, and he was worried. "Come over when you've got a moment. Have a little break."

She gave him a tired smile. "Okay."

But she came over a short while later, and hovered across the table from him, her hands on the chair. "We got a new shipment a few hours ago, and I've been rushing around putting everything in its place."

"Sit down, have a break," he told her.

"I can't," she said, glancing at her watch.

He folded the newspaper. "You're the boss. You can do anything you want."

"I suppose I can," she said, sitting down at the table.

He let out a sigh, feeling as if he could finally let loose. "I'm sick of it all," he said, rubbing his forehead, and folding the newspaper again.

"Sick of what?"

"Sick of …I don't even know. Roxy thinks I'm down because I hit thirty."

"Are you?"

"No." He peered closer. "Were you down? Have you hit thirty yet?"

"Not yet, I've still got a couple of months to go."

"And your boyfriend, has he hit thirty?"

"He's a couple of years older, but I doubt he'd have gotten upset about it. He doesn't think too deeply about these things."

"Wise man."

"I wouldn't say that."

"Shelly's coming this weekend," he told her, suddenly remembering.

"Is she definitely coming?"

He shrugged. "According to her latest call, but who knows? Tomorrow it could be a different story." His sister could be unpredictable like that.

He sighed loudly and squeezed the points below his eyebrows.

"Bad day?" Leigh asked.

"Not great."

"We all have not-so-great days."

"You don't," he retorted.

She laughed, and looked a little surprised. "I've had my share of bad days."

"You hide it well."

She pursed her lips together. "It becomes a skill if you do it enough times."

He wondered what she meant by that.

"Did you get any more of those notecards?" she asked, before he had a chance to ask her.

"Please, not you as well," he begged.

"What do you mean?"

"I'm so fed up with those darned love notes. I'm fed up with trying to figure out who they're from. Lately everyone seems to ask me that very same thing. I came here to get a break. "

"I'm sorry. I shouldn't have asked."

"Not you, Leigh. It's fine. I don't mind talking to you about it. The notes have stopped, and I'm glad," he told her. "They were starting to interfere with my work."

She stared at him blankly. "You didn't seem your usual self when I first saw you."

"I've had enough. You think they're romantic, but they're a pain in the butt." And he didn't want to talk about them anymore.

She cleared her throat while he took a sip of coffee. "How did you like the orange blossom muffin?" she asked.

"Good, but it's not a cinnamon bun."

Leigh grinned. "No, it's not."

"You know how I'm partial to those things as well as the—"

"Lemon drizzle," she cut in. "I know. Well, I'll be making those tomorrow as luck would have it."

"I should ask Dyson if he'd let me work here for half of my day every day. Set up my office here since I love the place so much."

"You say the nicest things about my bookstore."

"That's because you have the nicest bookstore."

CHAPTER 14

"*You're not sending it to him?*"

"*No.*"

"*Why not? You said you were having too much fun.*"

"*Not anymore.*"

Her friend pulled a chair out and sat down, her expression somber. "What happened?"

"*Nothing.*"

"*You'll have much more fun if you tell the guy how crazy you are about him.*"

"*I can't do that.*" *Her insides clamped tight. Whatever her feelings had been when she'd started this crazy thing, she knew now that she could never tell Rourke Halloran that she was madly, truly, deeper-than-the-ocean in love with him.*

She hadn't intended to do this.

Ever.

Ever.

Ever.

But she'd had a bad day when she'd sent the first one, and her romantic side had gotten the better of her. Now she had nothing but regrets about doing this.

"You're going to stop suddenly?"

"I am."

"And never tell him?"

"Never."

"But what happened?" her friend repeated.

"Nothing happened. I don't want to talk about it."

CHAPTER 15

"Tell him," Leigh begged. She'd turned up at Mackenzie's apartment to ask for a big favor.

Mackenzie's hands slipped to her hips, and she gave Leigh a hard stare. "You want *me* to tell him?"

"Yes."

Mackenzie opened her mouth to say something, but Leigh stood up and raised a hand, as if to silence her. "He's fed up of the notes. He said they're doing his head in, and that he can't concentrate. He said he's sick of trying to figure out who they're from. I'd rather not put him through that anymore."

"And whose fault is that? Certainly not mine," huffed Mackenzie. "When are you going to put him out of his misery, Leigh?"

She couldn't tell him. Rourke would cringe if he found out. Why, oh why, oh why had she done this? Mackenzie had warned her, and she herself knew this would happen, but she hadn't given it any proper thought.

She was a master at complicating her life, at attracting the losers, and then, chasing a man—albeit from a distance. Knowing she could never have him, but sending him love notes because her own life was so miserable and this sliver of light somehow made things a little easier.

It wasn't so easy now.

Rourke was irritated, and she had never wanted that.

"I wish I'd never done it." She fell onto the sofa in a huge, dramatic gesture. Propping her elbows on her knees, she covered her eyes with her hands. "It must have been the full moon, or something. Something that makes people go crazy. I don't know why I did it."

"You don't know why you did it?" Mackenzie asked, seating herself down next to her. "I do, you romantic fool."

"I can think of more appropriate words than fool." She heaved out another big sigh.

"Well?" Mackenzie asked. "Isn't it about time *you* put him out of his misery?"

"I can't." No way. No way at all. What worse thing could there be than to discover that someone you had no romantic ideas about was sending you romantic letters? She'd been insane to do it in the first place, but things hadn't gone so well for her in recent months. There had been that whole nasty business with Hank, her ex. She hadn't said a word to Rourke when he'd come into the bookshop the other day, making a nuisance of himself, being rude, and loud, and trashing *Doctor Zhivago*, one of her favorite romances, and making up news about a supposed new girlfriend. Rourke had no idea.

She'd maintained appearances. Kept up the pretense that she was still dating Hank, hoping that it would deflect suspicion away from her. From her daily interactions with Rourke, from those innocent conversations borne from years of friendship, something else seemed to flourish.

At least, for her.

Those briefly snatched moments with Rourke were an island of happiness in the shipwreck of her current life.

It wasn't that she was scarily obsessed with him, but her recent experiences with her ex-boyfriend had left her bruised and battered. No physical scars, only emotional ones. Rourke had been the light in all the darkness, and he hadn't even known it.

It was hard not to become used to that. Harder still, given that she'd always had a soft spot for her best friend's older brother over the years.

But now things had gotten out of hand.

"This can't go on, Leigh."

"I know." The poor man had looked more than annoyed when he had confided in her. She'd decided in that moment that she had to let him know. Merely stopping the notes wasn't going to cut it. She'd stopped them abruptly because what point was there in sending him the last one, especially after he'd told her that he suspected it might be Mackenzie, that he wanted it to be Mackenzie.

That had hurt. She'd tried her best to not let it, but it had.

It was impossible to be mad at Mackenzie . She was mostly mad at herself. "I don't know what came over me. It was fun, and he was so easy to talk to, and I …I never thought it would end up being this. A spaghetti storm of mixed feelings and emotions.

She hadn't been able to send that last note, but for him she would now. He wanted an end to it and she owed him that much. The chance for him to get closure.

Only, he would never know that she had been the one behind it all. "I can't tell him, Mackenzie, I can't."

"You can't tell him that you like him, but you have no problem sending him love letters?"

"It was only a few."

"Who does that in this day and age?"

"I didn't think about it too deeply." At the time she'd believed it would be romantic. Rourke often regaled her with his stories of his dates. Nothing crass. He'd come in and grab a cake and a latte and tell her that he'd met someone and that they didn't hit it off, and he was slowing down on his dating. But in recent months, he'd slowed right down. His stories about his exploits had waned.

Her own story had stopped months before Christmas, when she'd stood up to Hank. "It was supposed to be romantic," she said, her voice almost a whisper. "Something to cheer him up." And to cheer me up, she thought. In this digital age of dating sites and apps, where people met, sometimes for just one night, she wanted to reclaim a slice of the romance she read about in her books.

"Your head is too much in your books."

"It's an escape, and a wonderful one, at that. You should try it sometime." It was true. Her head was filled with the epic love stories she read, and she experience the same gut-wrenching emotion as the characters. That was the great thing about books. It was an escape from her reality, though her reality had taken a slightly dark turn with Hank, and she was doing her best to claw her way out of the pit.

"No, thank you."

Now Leigh was beginning to wish that she had never started any of this. "Please go and see him, Mackenzie, please. He thinks it's you, he *wants* it to be you."

"But it isn't me. It's you. I would never send out love notes to someone I was attracted to."

"I wasn't thinking."

"No, you weren't." Mackenzie walked towards her. "You've always had a soft spot for him."

She had. As her best friend's older brother, Rourke Halloran had caught her eye many a time. Too bad he'd never really noticed her. Most people didn't. She was used to that. It was only the losers whose attention she seemed to attract. People like Hank. She'd wanted to dream a little, wonder what it might be like to take a leap of faith and make a bold move so out of her comfort zone that it was like a trip to the moon. Rourke was out of her league. He was the kind of guy she would never ever get. But a girl could dream, couldn't she?

"I just wanted a bit of fun."

"The break-up with Hank was hard, I get it." Mackenzie sat down on the couch opposite Leigh. She'd never told Mackenzie the details, and had only said that she'd been sad about the break-up.

She hadn't been sad, she'd been relieved. What had left her feeling sad were his threatening text messages and the ones he left on her answering machine. Nobody knew about that, aside from Shelly, and she'd only told Shelly a fraction of the story.

But Rourke always made her laugh. cheered her up without even knowing every time he passed by the bookshop for his mid-afternoon coffee and cake. He told her he loved lemon drizzle loaves and her cinnamon buns and she'd started to make them regularly. He mentioned that he had to watch his weight and she'd started to look for low-calorie muffin and cookie recipes.

It was pathetic, but she liked doing tiny things like that because he made her forget Hank and all that ugliness. And, just like that, her early fascination with Shelly's gorgeous older brother resurfaced.

"This is your mess, Leigh, and you're going to have to clean it up."

She shook her head. "I can't."

She couldn't.

She could not go there.

How would she even begin to explain it to him? And where would she start? From Hank, or from Valentine's Day when Mackenzie's shop had been filled to bursting with red roses, and shops had been stocked with chocolates, and she'd had to set up a display table at the bookshop full of love-themed books.

It had been too much.

On a dare, and a whim, she'd penned a poem. Hastily made up. Well, not so hastily, but over the course of an afternoon, in between unboxing new books and overseeing the coffee and cake counter, she'd penned her four-line ode to Rourke. And she'd added her own little test to it.

She still hadn't sent out the fifth notecard, and had no intention of it. She doubted that he would even notice, and she would have left things as they were, but seeing him earlier today, and knowing she'd caused him this problem, made her want to come clean.

"If you can't, then I'll have to tell him for you," Mackenzie threatened.

"No, you can't," she begged, her insides turning to liquid at the thought of the humiliation. "He likes you, Mackenzie. He wants it to be you, and if you tell him it's you, that you were doing it on a dare then—"

"A dare?" Mackenzie looked at her in disbelief. "It's already sounding too complicated. Why can't you tell him?"

"Because he doesn't like me in that way."

"My goodness, Leigh! You want me to pretend I like him, when I don't? What if he likes me?"

"He does."

"But I don't like him, not like that. You really didn't think this through, did you?"

She took a deep breath in. Of course she hadn't. She hadn't been in a good place back then. It had been something light and daring, and fun. They stared at one another. Then Leigh shook her head. "He'll get over it. He likes women, and then he forgets about them. Easy come, easy go."

"If he likes women, why don't you tell him your feelings for him and see what he says?"

"Rourke's never noticed me. He never would." Girls like Mackenzie didn't understand that. "I'd die of embarrassment if I told him it was me. He doesn't see me as … as girlfriend material."

"How do you know when you haven't given him the benefit of the doubt?"

"We're just friends. There's not a chance of anything happening between us." It was one-sided, this attraction she had for him. Hank had always told her she was plain and average. He'd hated that she owned and managed the bookshop, and he'd never been able to understand why she didn't just get a job working for someone else. He called her a leech when she once asked him to lend her some money because her cash flow was tight, even though she'd told him she'd pay him back in a few weeks' time.

She never asked after that, after he called her a bloodsucking leech, and conveniently forgot that whenever they went out to watch a movie or get takeout, that she was the one who paid. "I've always had a thing for Rourke, since I was a teenager, but a guy like that is out of my league. He thinks you're gorgeous."

Leigh saw Mackenzie roll her eyes, and brush away the flurry of curls that had fallen over her shoulder. She could see exactly why Rourke wished it was Mackenzie. What red-blooded man in his right mind wouldn't wish for a woman like that?

Mackenzie came over to her. Bending down until her face was level with Leigh's, she said, "I told you, when you sent the second notecard, that this could go wrong. Now, what, four notecards later? Things are clearly going wrong. Don't make it worse, Leigh. Tell him now."

Leigh shook her head ferociously. "That's not going to happen, Mackenzie. I can't do that. I didn't think it through, you're right, but I wasn't thinking straight back then. I can't take it all back. I can't just leave him dangling. It's the not knowing that's bugging him."

"And you think me lying to him is going to make things easier?"

"Seeing Rourke all riled up makes me want to set the record straight, but I can't tell him. I *won't* tell him." She ran through the scene in her head, of her telling Rourke and him laughing. She couldn't go through with seeing the shock explode across his face. He'd expected Mackenzie to be his secret admirer and if he found out that it was her instead, he would be terribly disappointed. She didn't want to be a disappointment to him. It was bad enough that Hank had told her plenty of times that she was a waste of space. Tears welled up at the reminder of those words. "Please don't make me. You don't know how he talked about you. How much he wanted it to be you."

"It's not right, Leigh—"

She put up her hand to silence her friend. "I know that, but I'm choosing to be kind, not right." Mackenzie didn't know what it was like to not get noticed. Forcing someone to like you, to see you, wasn't the basis of a great romance.

"Are you crying?" Mackenzie's face softened. "Leigh," she crooned, getting on her knees now. "Hey, what's going on?" She pressed her shoulder gently. "Don't get upset."

"I'm not upset," she insisted, but her heart was heavy, and she felt as if she had lost something big, something precious, something irreplaceable..

"You look like you're going to cry. Are you that crazy about him?"

"No. No, I swear." She wasn't *that* crazy about Rourke. She wasn't an airy-fairy love-struck teenager. She'd only been with Hank for a few months before she'd seen his true colors, but those few months had been enough for him to dismantle her self-esteem. She was only now picking up the pieces and putting herself back together again. Nobody else knew. Everyone thought she had her life together. That she was hard-working and cheerful, and she was, hard-working, because it forced her not to dwell on the dark stuff. As for being cheerful, anyone could wear a mask.

Mackenzie lowered her head and shook it, then looked at her. "Okay. I'll do it."

She released a sigh of relief. "You will? Are you sure?"

"I'm sure."

"Thank you." Once this was done, she would put it all behind her. "I'm sorry to ask you for this. I know it's a huge favor."

"Huge." Mackenzie smiled. "You'll have to bake me a whole double loaf cake to make up for it."

"Done."

CHAPTER 16

"Are you free this weekend?" Shelly asked. "I'm definitely coming down this time."

"I'm not sure." Leigh hesitated. At any other time this would have been a great opportunity to meet with her best friend, but right now the timing sucked.

"If you're busy, we can meet for a coffee?" Shelly suggested, somehow sensing Leigh's hesitation. "I can come over to the bookshop, and we can catch up."

"Uh…sure."

"Saturday? Around noon?"

"That works for me." Especially because Rourke never came to the bookshop during the weekend.

"See you then."

Leigh hung up, and although she wanted to meet up with her friend, she felt out of sorts about meeting Rourke's sister. Shelly would think she was insane if she ever found out that Leigh had sent Rourke those notes.

Luckily, Rourke hadn't come by the bookshop in the past few days, which was a good thing, because she wasn't sure how she would react if he did. She'd written another love note and given it to Mackenzie, for the 'revelation' –whenever that would be.

She wanted this episode to be forgotten. Soon there would be something else going on in Starling Bay, and she wouldn't have to worry about this. The most recent talk of the town had been about Reed Knight; something to do with him and the maid who used to work for him. But even that wasn't such a big deal any more, though it had been a few months ago when everyone had thought that the maid had caused the break-up between Reed and his fiancée. But Reed's interview in the local paper had put things right.

There was talk that Hailey Ross was heading back to Starling Bay. Rumors were that she was going to make a documentary about her rise to Hollywood from her humble beginnings in Starling Bay. Perhaps that would be the next story to dominate the headlines here this summer.

She was upstairs, arranging one of the display tables, when she heard him. Even from a floor away, even when she wasn't on the same level as him, she could somehow tell when Rourke was in the shop. He wasn't particularly loud, but his voice, in this instance, reached her ears. She'd read about this phenomenon, that being attracted to someone made you sense them, hear them, and feel them, even from afar.

He looked around, then up, and she stepped back, out of his line of sight. Hiding from him.

He ordered something from the cake counter then left. That was when she called Mackenzie.

Rourke left the bookshop and found it odd that he hadn't seen Leigh around.

As he walked back towards work, Mackenzie was outside her

store, looking at it from across the narrow street. She crossed over and peered into the window again.

"Hey," he said, nodding. "What are you doing?"

"Taking a look at my display. What do you think of it?"

He looked at the bright yellow flowers in the window, and the display made up of Easter bunnies, baskets and Easter eggs. His mouth fell open. "That's incredible."

"That's exactly the response I was looking for."

"No, but seriously." He stared at it again, unable to take his eyes off it. "That's brilliant. You did this?"

She nodded.

Wow. This gorgeous beauty was a creative genius, as well as a business woman. She was the whole package.

"I …I have something for you," she said, her voice suddenly wavering. "Would you mind coming inside? It won't take long."

That piqued his interest. He followed her in.

She walked towards her table, then strode up to him with something in her hand. "For you."

"What's that—" And then he saw the familiar little white envelope.

His breath escaped him.

Mackenzie?

Mackenzie was behind the love notes?

"I was supposed to send this a few weeks ago, but …" she looked embarrassed. "I felt silly towards the end. I couldn't bring myself to mail this one."

He was too speechless and too shocked to react.

"Aren't you going to say something?" she asked.

"You?" he gasped. Even though he had suspected it might be her, having her confess to him like this while handing him another note seemed too much to take in.

"I'm sorry. I didn't mean to spring this on you. I feel silly owning up to it."

"Why are you?" he asked, curious. He had once thought that it might be Mackenzie, but having her confess it now seemed too easy, too straightforward. It didn't feel right.

"I…I thought I should. I mean… " She swiped her hand over her forehead. "This isn't easy. I almost didn't want to tell you but I felt it was the right thing to do." She looked over his shoulder. "I have to take care of the customers, please, would you excuse me?"

She walked away, leaving him to read the card:

> *This was fun, this escape,*
> *this momentary madness.*
> *But for you was it the same,*
> *Or was it sheer gladness?*

Something was different about this one, it seemed final, like a goodbye. It had none of the feeling, the hint of sadness that the others had. Perhaps he was reading too much into the four lines. He re-read it again, and wasn't sure what to make of it.

Mackenzie returned. "It is cringe-worthy," she said, looking pained as he stared at the note. "It started off as a joke, I mean, it was around Valentine's Day, and we'd had this stunning display in the window, and everywhere I looked were baskets of red roses, and I …uh…" She sighed loudly as if the explanation of it all was a chore. "I got carried away. I'm sorry."

'*I'm sorry*' didn't sound like the right expression. What was she being sorry about? That she had imposed herself on him, derailed his thoughts, hijacked his emotional energy? Or was she apologizing for being attracted to him?

Did she find him cute? Did she do it on a dare? Did she like him? He didn't know what to say, or what to feel, because he was numb. It wasn't the ecstatic reaction he had imagined when his secret admirer finally revealed her identity, and as much as he had wished it to be Mackenzie, his wish now coming true didn't have the 'wow' factor he had imagined it might.

"I'm…flattered," he said, curious about her intentions, before and now.

He didn't know Mackenzie well, and this revelation made him uncomfortable. He wondered if this was what women felt like when they were hit on by a man they didn't know, for no reason than good looks. "I don't know what to say."

"I've put you in a difficult situation."

"No, no you haven't." He forced a laugh. What was the matter with him? A drop-dead gorgeous woman had confessed to sending him the notecards. Why wasn't he jumping like a jubilant bunny?

"I was foolish. I didn't mean anything by it, and…and I just want you to know that I…I was…I used to get a kick out of seeing your reaction."

"A kick?" he asked, frowning. She was having a hard time explaining, and he was having a hard time understanding.

"Look, Rourke, you're a great-looking guy, but I barely know you. Let's just put it down to one crazy moment when I was feeling blue. I didn't have a Valentine's Day date, and I …I did it on the spur-of the moment, without thinking. I just wanted to let you know, in case you thought that I might be crazy about you… because I'm not, okay? Let's just get that straight."

"You're not?" he asked, feeling relieved for some reason he didn't understand.

"You're a nice guy, but I'm not…I'm not interested in you that way. And I know it was a silly thing to do to send those things to you when I didn't have those thoughts, but…" She groaned. "This is really hard."

"I can see you're having a hard time telling me."

"I'm sorry."

"Please, stop apologizing."

"It was a childish thing to do."

"Let's leave it at that, shall we?" He knew now, and he could put this matter to rest. What he didn't understand was the disappointment gnawing at his gut. He should have been elated, yet curiously, he wasn't.

CHAPTER 17

She was going around the top floor of the bookshop, turning out the lights when Mackenzie flounced in. She looked flustered, and Leigh could tell that she'd told Rourke.

"I'm up here," she shouted. Mackenzie charged up the stairs. "So?" she asked, breathlessly, her eyes wide like saucers waiting for Mackenzie to speak.

"I told him. It's done."

"Thanks. I feel bad that I made you do that." She could understand asking Shelly to cover for her, but asking Mackenzie, a new friend, seemed to be pushing it. She was going to bake her double chocolate loaf cake and take it over to her later tonight.

"Don't ever make me do anything like that again."

"I won't. I promise. How bad was it?"

"Worse than awful. I had to lie through my teeth. Poor guy. I felt so bad lying to him."

Leigh leaned against the bannister. "I don't understand why. He wanted it to be you."

"You say that, but what if he didn't want it to be me? What if he changed his mind when it came down to it? I felt bad for lying."

Shock slammed into her like a juggernaut. What if Mackenzie really liked Rourke but now had to pretend she didn't, because she knew Leigh did. "Do you like him?"

"No. I felt bad for lying to him. Now he thinks I sent those notes. It was embarrassing for both of us."

"You gave him the new notecard?"

"I did everything you told me to."

"And?"

"He wanted to know why I was confessing now."

Had he believed her? She would have expected him to be relieved, happy even. After all, it was the whole reason she had forced Mackenzie to make the confession in the first place otherwise she couldn't have even sent the fifth note. As it was, the note she'd given Mackenzie wasn't the original one she had intended to send him.

Not that it mattered any more. "Didn't he say anything else, about how he'd suspected that it might be you?"

"No." Mackenzie paced around the top landing, her body a swirling movement of long limbs and long hair. "He looked embarrassed."

"He said you were gorgeous," Leigh insisted. "He wanted it to be you."

"It's done, I just wanted you to know that it was over with."

"It was a huge thing to ask of you, and I'm grateful to you for doing this for me. Thank you."

"I'd like extra chocolate in my cake," said Mackenzie, getting ready to go down the stairs.

"I'm baking it tonight. I can bring it over when it's fresh out of the oven?"

"That might make this seem worthwhile," replied Mackenzie.

"I'll be over later." Shelly was also coming down on the weekend. It wasn't ideal, but at least the love note drama was done with. She was still curious to know about Rourke, though. "He didn't even ask you out on a date?"

"No."

"That's good, isn't it? I mean, you don't like him, do you?"

"I don't like him, not in that way, but I felt sorry for him, that he might think I *did* like him. Let's face it, why else would I send out those notes in the first place?"

She and Mackenzie had gone over the different scenarios yesterday of what Mackenzie would say to Rourke in case he thought she liked him.

Leigh's worst fear had been that Rourke would ask Mackenzie on a date, and that Mackenzie might have liked him but would have felt obliged to say no because she knew Leigh had a soft spot for him. Not that Leigh would ever have confessed anything to Rourke. That man would never know.

"I felt sorry for him," Mackenzie continued. Leigh opened her mouth to say something, but there was nothing to say. Her friend had done exactly as she had asked, and Rourke had the end result he wanted, even if nothing would come from it.

In a few weeks' time this would be old news.

CHAPTER 18

*M*ackenzie.

A week ago he would have been ecstatic to discover that it was her, but the discovery had been something of an anti-climax and he couldn't figure out why.

The tall and striking florist was his ideal woman, so why didn't he feel more enthused when she had confessed?

Maybe this was just another symptom of the continued malaise he'd felt in recent months, partly brought on by the big three-O. It was also having an impact on his dating life. He'd slowed right down with regards to women.

On a normal day, he would have called his friends and asked them to meet him at the Blue Velvet Bar so that he could tell them. But his mood was subdued, and he couldn't explain why. Besides, Dylan was probably with Merry, and Reed with Jenna. He was hesitant to encroach on their time, but he also wasn't sure what to make of Mackenzie's confession. It had been a joke, she'd told him. She'd done it for a joke, and she didn't really like him like that. That's what she'd said.

So he went home, fixed himself a microwaved dinner, then sat down in front of the TV, flicking through the channels looking for something to distract him. But his mind kept coming back to the conversation with Mackenzie.

He pulled out the notecard from his briefcase and read it again, and then he pulled out the other four and laid them all out on the sofa, reading them for the last time, knowing that Mackenzie had been behind them.

There was only one thing to do with them now; put them through his document shredder.

It had been silly and childish. He sensed that Mackenzie had felt the same. She had been embarrassed and had struggled to own up to it. He'd been partly embarrassed for her; after all, they weren't love-struck teens. Grown-ups didn't do this kind of stuff, though, he had to admit, at first he'd found it romantic. It was different than the dating apps he was used to, and his usual way of meeting women by going up to them in bars, getting their numbers, hitting on them.

For a brief moment, he'd been sucked in by these subtle and cute notes.

His gaze flitted over the last poem. It was written in the same handwriting, but felt rushed.

He slumped back on the sofa, his arms lifted and behind his head, as he stared up at the ceiling and contemplated the state of things. Shelly was coming over, so he needed to make up the spare room for her, and get some food in. She told him she'd already made a dinner reservation at Fellini's for the both of them.

Should he mention the love notes to his sister? Should he tell her about Mackenzie, the florist and the wonderful story behind the name, Bloom?

Be Like the One and Only Mackenzie.

Sweet.

Smart.

Clever.

Maybe not.

The shredder was the best place for these because he didn't want his sister to set eyes on them. She wouldn't stop teasing him about them.

He was about to gather up the notecards when his gaze wandered from each poem in order, from the first to the fifth. And then his gaze went back to the first and he re-read them all again.

He saw something he'd missed before.

He jumped up off the sofa, shock slamming into him like a truck.

L.E.I.G, that's what the first letters of each of the first four poems spelled out.

Leigh?

It was freaky.

It had to be a pure coincidence, didn't it?

His brow furrowed as the jigsaw slotted into place.

The fifth poem was odd, but he'd already sensed that. It should have begun with H, if his theory was right, except that it hadn't. At least, the note Mackenzie gave him hadn't.

Leigh was the one behind the notecards?

His friend, Leigh.

No, *Shelly's* friend Leigh.

His little sister's best friend?

He raked his hands through his hair, wondering if this crazy theory of his might have some substance to it, or whether it was a sheer fluke.

What was the chance of those letters spelling out a name? Something had gone awry with the fifth note. It had been late, and it hadn't started like all the others, and Mackenzie had confessed in an awkward and uneasy confession.

That's why this recent notecard had been different—because it wasn't the one Leigh had intended to send. This was why the fifth note looked odd, and why Mackenzie owned up, and why she felt so pained and uncomfortable. He'd told Leigh he wanted it to be

Mackenzie... and that was why the fifth love note hadn't come on time.

It started to make sense.

It wasn't Mackenzie at all.

It was Leigh. He thought back to their recent conversations and interactions at the bookshop, small pieces slowly starting to make sense. To fit.

Oh, the ruse, the ruse, the ruse.

All the lengths she had gone to, to hide her identity from him.

But, she had a boyfriend. She did, most definitely. Or that was what she'd told him. There was only one way to find out.

He called Shelly, needing evidence, a hint, or a sign as he tried to piece it all together.

"Hey, just making sure you're still coming down on Friday. You keep changing your plans so…"

"I'm definitely coming. I've got to do it before you turn thirty-one."

"Ha-ha. Very funny."

"We've got dinner reservations on Saturday night, but I'm seeing Leigh for brunch first thing."

"You are?" Fancy that. "I knew you'd try and fit everyone in. We can do lunch on Sunday as well, before you head back."

"Sounds cool."

"Oh," he tried to sound nonchalant about it. "It will be nice for you two to catch up. She's still with that boyfriend, isn't she?" He couldn't remember his name, Leigh had mentioned it a while back. He tried to sound vague, as if this piece of intel wasn't important.

"Hank?"

Ah, Hank. It sounded familiar. "Yeah, Hank."

Shelly didn't say anything for a few seconds, then, "Why?"

Not the answer he was expecting. "No reason. We were just talking, about getting older, and she mentioned he was older."

"They broke up about six months ago. But I suppose you don't know that."

Huh?

This was not the answer he'd been expecting, but it was the answer that made perfect sense.

"They broke up," he repeated, trying to hide the surprise.

"Some nasty stuff went on between them. Leigh doesn't like talking about it."

"What kind of nasty stuff?"

"I can't say, Rourke. You're not supposed to know. She doesn't want anyone to know."

"Is she okay?"

"Yes. The guy was a jerk, that's all I'm going to say."

He thought about that, and how Leigh had kept up appearances, telling him she was still with him.

"Promise me you won't say a word to her," his sister begged.

"I won't."

But the evidence was mounting, and this was all the proof he needed to know that Leigh had been behind the notecards. "See you on Saturday."

"I'll come over to your place and drop my luggage before I see Leigh."

"I'd better freshen up the spare room."

He hung up and drew out a long breath, trying to process all that he had just discovered.

Given what he now knew, everything slotted in perfectly.

There was no doubt about it. Leigh was his secret admirer, except that she was still intent on keeping it hidden. She'd gone to the trouble of asking her friend to lie for her. He understood now why she had done that, as he recalled the time he'd bought flowers from Bloom then given them to Leigh, and then told her he suspected that it was Mackenzie.

That was why she had made Mackenzie pretend.

But oddly, unlike the time of Mackenzie's revelation, he didn't feel uncomfortable at this new revelation. He felt flattered, and curious, but not repelled by the idea.

In fact, he felt curiously *good.*

Leigh had never been on his radar before because she had always been Shelly's friend. He'd never had any other place for her other than to class her as his sister's friend.

Leigh had tried so hard to hide her tracks, even going so far as to fabricate the story that she was still with Hank. And the cinnamon buns and lemon drizzle loaves she made, and then the low-calorie muffins and cookies she'd trialed after he'd complained that he needed to watch his weight.

She had listened to him, and she had acted on it. He suddenly felt warm and looked after.

And now he understood why she'd stayed away when he'd come to the bookshop this week. She had been deliberately avoiding him.

Putting himself in her shoes, he clearly understood why. Especially after he'd told her that he so much wanted it to be Mackenzie. He felt like a douchebag for putting her through that.

But now that he knew, what should he do? Was he going to approach her?

Going up to her and telling her that he knew wasn't the way to go about it. He sensed she was probably already dying from the humiliation of sending those love notes.

Or should he confront Mackenzie? But that wouldn't be any good either. Mackenzie would tell Leigh, and he sensed she didn't want this secret to come out.

There had to be another way.

CHAPTER 19

"Hey." He tried to sound normal, tried to keep himself from staring into her face too much. He had to make a concerted effort to do so.

He'd come at a time he wouldn't normally have come, early in the morning, before he went into work. But he had wanted to see Leigh before the place got busy, before she got busy with people.

"Hi." Knowing what he did, her muted reaction now made more sense.

"I need some caffeine to get me started today."

"You're early," she noted. Her face was red, and she looked flustered. He hoped it wasn't because he'd suddenly turned up and made her feel uncomfortable, because that was something he didn't want. He wanted to get back to how things were between them before, to their easy camaraderie, to their effortless banter, and conversation.

It had only been a day since he'd found out, but already the change between them was like the tip of an iceberg. On the surface of it, they were polite enough and Leigh's smile was warm, but it didn't reach her eyes.

Deep down, things had shifted. She was being guarded and he couldn't reach in.

"I found out who my secret admirer is."

Her eyelids flew open, and she stared at him. "Who?"

"Mackenzie."

"Mackenzie?" she said, her face displaying all the elements of surprise that he had come to know so well. Looking at her this morning, he was seeing the old Leigh, but with new eyes. "Huh," she made a questioning sound, then pried open the lids to her plastic containers. He eyed them with anticipation knowing that these were the cakes she baked for him. He prayed for lemon drizzle.

"Yeah, I know," he said, nodding, "Hard to believe, huh?"

"Hard to believe? You guessed right. Aren't you glad?"

"Glad?"

"You wanted it to be her, didn't you?"

"Well, yeah, I guess, but—"

"But what?"

"I don't know her."

"So, you can get to know her."

"I know you better."

She let out a small surprised gasp. "Maybe."

"Maybe? Leigh, you and I have history. We go back years."

"I suppose, but that's only because you're Shelly's brother."

"Only because I'm Shelly's brother?" he looked her squarely in the eye, before moving his face closer, and dropping his voice—the effect worked, he'd tested it on dozens of women—"Only because I'm Shelly's brother, Leigh? You and I are friends regardless of that stuff."

Another tiny gasp escaped her lips.

He liked this, toying with her and observing her reaction. And her reaction to this was sheer confusion. He wondered what she might be thinking. He couldn't hint too much, not yet, better to play it subtle for now. "You give me an escape from work stuff."

"You've helped me with my business plans and funding," she said.

"See? And Shelly had nothing to do with any of that."

Leigh cleared her throat. "But Mackenzie is stunning, absolutely gorgeous. Any man would be flattered to know that someone like her was interested in him."

"Sure. She's a looker, can't deny that. It's just…"

"Just what?"

He raked a hand through his hair, "Just that I can't… I don't know."

"Don't know what?"

"I don't know what it means."

Her mouth fell open, slightly. "What did Mackenzie say?"

"She said she didn't mean it seriously. It was a joke, when she was bored and lonely on Valentine's Day."

"She said that?" Leigh asked, looking genuinely surprised. She was good at this game-playing, and he was happy to play along. For now. His stomach did a happy dance as she pulled out a loaf of lemon drizzle cake. "I'll have a slice of that, please."

"You're not counting calories today?"

"Not today."

She cut out a thick slice of cake for him. "Anything else?"

"And a coffee, to go." He'd done his bit for the morning. "So, I guess that's the end of it. No more love notes."

"You sound disappointed," she remarked.

"They were fun to get."

"That's not what you said last time when you sounded fed up about it."

"I know who sent them now, and even though Mackenzie and I aren't really attracted to each other, I'm happy now that I at least know who sent them."

Leigh handed him over the coffee and he gave her the money. "It must be nice knowing the secret is out."

"And what a secret it was, right?" He wasn't sure if he was imagining it or whether Leigh actually blushed when he said that.

He could see now why sending those cards could be addictive. It was an exciting game, being at the other end of a secret. He'd been at the receiving end of Leigh's little game and secret, but now the tables had turned, and he liked his new position.

CHAPTER 20

*L*eigh rushed into The Olive Tree restaurant and found Shelly sitting at a table waiting.

"Sorry I'm late," she said, as they hugged.

"I only just got here myself," Shelly told her.

"We had a new delivery of books, and I got caught up."

"I thought that hiring extra staff was supposed to free you up more."

"It has," said Leigh, sitting down and looking at the menu. "But there's always something to do. Anyway, you look well," she said, admiring Shelly's perfectly coiffed hair and makeup. She was always immaculately put together. The Halloran siblings had a passing resemblance, and both were always perfectly groomed.

She smoothed down her hair; she'd rushed out this morning and hadn't brushed it properly. As it was, she usually had it in a ponytail, which didn't bother her much, unless Rourke was coming by the bookshop. But now, next to Shelly, she felt a little scruffy.

The bookshop was closed on Sundays, and she tried not to work on Saturdays, but Books & Buns, being her own business, she had ended up working six days for most weeks. She had tried to come in just for an hour, to make sure everything was running smoothly, but it usually ended up swallowing up her entire day.

The irony of her meeting Shelly today of all days wasn't lost on her, but she pushed everything about Rourke to the side and focused instead on Shelly and her new job. Then Leigh told her about her recent goings-on, about life at the bookshop and how easier things had been ever since she'd learned to delegate more.

"You're taking Rourke to Fellini's for dinner?" she asked, hoping to elicit some information from Shelly about her brother.

"He doesn't want to celebrate. He's in denial about turning thirty. I couldn't come when he celebrated with our parents—I was away for a week, meeting a client, but even with me coming to see him now, he said I was making a huge fuss about it."

Leigh knew. All this weight-watching, or apparent wish to watch his weight, was new. Rourke talked about it more than he adhered to it, seeing that he hadn't really taken to her low-calorie selection at the cake counter. "He seems to be having a hard time of it," agreed Leigh. She always looked forward to his visits to the bookshop, and it had been hard avoiding him at the bookshop this last week. His sudden and unexpected early morning appearance a few days ago had taken her by surprise.

"But he was in a good mood this morning," Shelly said, turning the menu over. "Happier than I've seen him lately, and I don't think it was because I showed up."

"Maybe he sold a property or something," Leigh offered. "Your brother likes his commission checks."

"True. He is working on a gazillion dollar property on the other side of the bay. Mansions that huge take time to sell, though. I'm not sure it's anything to do with work. I think he might have his eyes on a new love interest."

"What makes you say that?" she asked, as her stomach

bottomed out. But she already knew. He was no doubt happy to have discovered the truth about Mackenzie. However, this news didn't fit in with Mackenzie's version of how her confession had been received. It now left Leigh wondering if her friend had played down Rourke's reaction so as not to hurt her feelings. She wondered the same about Rourke's muted reaction when he'd told her that he'd found out it was Mackenzie.

"Because I know my brother. I know when his mind's on work stuff, because he gets all serious and distracted about it, and I know when it's other stuff, like a new girlfriend, because he can't think straight. And he has this stupid grin on his face most of the time when he doesn't realize people are looking."

Leigh's insides heaved. She'd been hungry this morning, and had been looking forward to brunch at The Olive Tree, but this news turned her insides upside down.

And it shouldn't have, because she wasn't even with Rourke. He had only ever been a fantasy, someone on whom she'd had a crush on from afar. The fact that she now felt a stab of pain at this news was purely her fault, and the fault of those darned love notes.

Of course Rourke was happy. Mackenzie was stunning, and she was probably everything Rourke wanted in a woman. The two of them made the perfect couple, a gorgeous guy like him, and a model-looking woman like Mackenzie, there was bound to be attraction between them. The thought slapped her like one of Hank's cruel put-downs.

"And what about you?" Shelly asked. "Anyone new in your life?"

Leigh felt her body sag as she sat back, feeling winded. "I don't get the chance to meet anyone, I'm in the bookshop nearly every day of the week. Sunday is for inventory and going through the figures. You know me, I practically live in this place."

"How are you doing?" asked Shelly, the innocent question loaded.

"Fine," replied Leigh, braving a smile.

"Have you seen him lately?"

Although she didn't refer to him by name, Leigh knew who she meant. "He's come by the bookshop a couple of times."

"And…?"

"He's usually been fine. I'm busy most of the time so I don't have to deal with him but the last time he came he was downright nasty."

"Nasty?" Shelly looked worried. "You need to tell someone, maybe even report it to the police."

She didn't want to make things worse. Hank hadn't ever hit her. He'd never been physically abusive. He was just a messed up and confused man, and her decision to split had obviously hurt him. "He'll calm down," she replied. She was sure of it. "I don't want to ruin our meal talking about him. He's not worth it. Tell me about your new job. Have you met any hot young lawyers?"

CHAPTER 21

It was sweet, Shelly treating him to dinner at Fellini's for his birthday, and giving him a pair of silver cufflinks for a present.

His kid sister was doing well with her new job at a law firm in New York. They'd caught up with one another regarding their jobs, and stresses, and life in general. He let her know about Dylan and Reed and their change in status. She had initially suggested asking them along to dinner as well, but he had insisted he didn't want to make a big thing about his birthday, even though this was just a dinner.

He much preferred the quiet dinner with Shelly.

"You met with Leigh earlier?" he asked, as they dug into their main meal.

"We went to that restaurant in The Grand Hotel, you know the one where mom likes to go for brunch, The Olive Tree."

He wasn't so interested in where they'd gone to eat. "Did you check out the bookshop? She's had the café refurbed."

"She showed me after. It's so cool! We had coffee and cake there."

"She's done a great job with that place," he said, feeling

immensely proud of her all of a sudden. He'd helped her draw up the business plan and helped her with her loan for the coffee corner.

"What happened with her boyfriend?"

Shelly looked uneasy for a second. "She…they… just… split up."

Though he now understood why Leigh had gone to such long lengths to keep up the pretense of their relationship, he was curious. "I know they split up, but what happened?"

"I can't say, Rourke. Please don't ask me. Leigh doesn't want to talk about it."

He didn't like the sound of that.

"She's never let on, you know? She's always pretended they were still together."

"I don't know why. She's a private person, she doesn't volunteer information easily."

"She's volunteered those lies easily enough."

"I don't know why," his sister replied.

"Have you ever met him?"

"Never. But she always used to say he had a bit of a nasty streak in him."

"Nasty?" Rourke's stomach steeled. "He hit her?"

"No, no. Nothing like that, he just wasn't nice to her. Treated her like she was a dumbass, and she's not. She's smart."

"She is smart." His eyes were slowly beginning to open, and it was as if he was seeing her for the first time. She was smart, and funny, and caring. She had always been around when he'd needed someone to talk to. He didn't want any of that to change.

"I don't want to say anymore. Leigh didn't want anyone to know."

"She's making low-calorie healthy stuff for the café."

"I know. She told me. She credits you with that."

He grinned. "I might have casually mentioned that I have to watch what I'm eating now."

"Not the moment you turn thirty, Rourke! Leigh and I really do think you aren't handling this well—growing older gracefully."

"You were talking about me?" This was interesting, and uplifting. "What did she say?"

"About what? About you?" Shelly looked at him, puzzled for a moment. "She didn't say much, except that you didn't seem to be handling turning thirty well."

"That's not true," he replied defiantly. He wasn't having any such problems. He wasn't.

"Not true, says the man who refused to celebrate it."

Unknowingly, Shelly had given him a brainwave of an idea. He *was* going to have a party, and he was going to get Roxy to do the catering, and he would ask Leigh to bake the cake. She would think he was crazy, or she might begin to suspect that he knew— for she wasn't a baker by trade, and she would wonder why he didn't get the cake from a professional bakery, but heck, her lemon drizzle loaves were to die for and he loved that she still baked those herself.

He was going to ask her to make the cake and then somewhere between asking her and before the party, he would confront her with the news that he knew it was her and not Mackenzie. Not confront her as in demand an explanation, for he figured that Leigh didn't want him to know, but he couldn't *not* tell her. He couldn't let the lie live.

Right now, he wasn't sure why he needed Leigh to know that he had figured it out. What he did know was that he wasn't disappointed to discover she had been behind it all. He had never had anyone be interested in him and show it in such an old-fashioned way.

It was sweet.

Heck, he'd never had women hitting on him before, he was always used to doing the chasing.

There had been a touch of mystery around the love notes, and he had enjoyed that, at first, anyway. He wasn't sure about his feelings for Leigh, because this was all so different for him. She wasn't his type, for starters, she wasn't tall, or super-slim, but she had a beautiful face, heart-shaped, and she never needed any make-up. He liked that. But he hadn't really looked at her like that before. He'd only ever seen the person she was underneath, her heart, her soul, the way she was, cheery and happy, and always going out of her way to make things better for others—customers, yes, but she went the extra mile. She had heart.

She was his sister's friend, and he'd never thought of her as girlfriend material before, but he was already starting to see her in a new light.

"You've twisted my arm. I'm going to do it."

"What?"

"I'm going to have a party."

"Yay!" Shelly clapped her hands together lightly. "Better late than never."

He nodded, not entirely sure why he'd made this crazy move, but thoughts swirled around in his head. Why not have a simple party at his place? A few friends, and work friends, and Shelly, and Leigh. The people who mattered. He wasn't sure where he was going with it, but it was too late to take it back. The party was on.

"Where? And how many people?"

"Don't go getting excited," he told her, "otherwise I'll change my mind. It's going to be small, and it's going to be at my place."

"When? I need to make sure I'm free."

"How about you consult your diary, and let me know when I can have my party?" he asked, grinning.

The smell of freshly baked cake and coffee, and the early morning quietness of the bookshop reeled him in. Leigh was over by the book service counter taking out books from a box.

"Hey, Good morning," he said, sounding extremely upbeat.

Leigh looked up, her expression slightly downcast. "Good morning. We're not open yet."

"But your door was open," he countered.

"I wasn't expecting any customers yet." He wasn't sure what to make of her slightly edgy demeanor. "Shall I come back later?"

She stopped what she was doing, then shook her head, looking apologetic. "Of course not."

He stepped away, not wanting to pressure her into anything. "I can come back later."

"Stay. It's only you." She smiled.

"It's only me, Leigh. What's up? Bad weekend? Did my sister get on your nerves?" he was trying to make her laugh.

Her lips twisted for a moment, as if she were about to say something, then, "Shelly never gets on my nerves. It was great to catch up with her." She pulled out a stack of books from the box. "How was your meal?"

"Awesome, as to be expected," he replied, watching as she reached for the next box and started taking books out. Had she had coffee? And breakfast? Or did she just get to work and get on with work right away?

"Want me to help you with that?" he asked, seeing that he was just standing here doing nothing but getting in her way.

She laughed. "No, of course not. You're the customer, Rourke."

"I'm a friend first."

She angled her head at that but said nothing.

"And you're not open yet, you said so yourself."

She grinned as she opened the next box with a letter opener. "Thanks, but I've got this."

"How about I help you with that, and you get it done quicker, then we can both sit down and have breakfast. I bet you haven't had breakfast yet, have you?"

She looked at him as if he'd grown another nose. Maybe he was coming on too strong with his offer of help.

"It's okay, really. I'll serve you in a moment, as soon as I've done this."

"No rush," he told her, content to stay here and do nothing but talk.

"Shelly said you were really happy to see her."

He snorted. "She said that?"

"Well, she said you seemed really happy. She seems to think it's because you've met someone."

It surprised him, that Leigh and Shelly had been discussing his love life. He wondered if Leigh had told his sister about the love notes. Curious to know, he asked, "Why were you and my sister talking about my nonexistent love life?" He made a point to mention that it was nonexistent. Leigh already knew that, because he'd often, in the past, talked about places and restaurants he'd been to on a date, and if it had been a particularly nice place, he'd mention it to her. Lately, he'd had nothing to talk about in that respect.

"*We* weren't," she pointed out. "It was your sister who made that comment."

"There's definitely no girlfriend."

She glanced at him, now that the second box was empty and two piles of books were neatly stacked nearby. "Mackenzie didn't cheer you up?"

"Mackenzie put me out of my misery," he said carefully, suddenly piecing together where her earlier frostiness might have come from, "but there is no new woman in my life."

"You're showing up earlier and earlier," she said, cleverly directing the conversation to another place.

"I can't keep away from this place," he replied truthfully.

A tiny smile appeared on her lips. "How come?" she asked, bending down and disappearing entirely from view.

"How come what?"

She popped back up again with a book and a calculator. "How come you're here so early these days?"

"Would you rather I didn't come?"

"No," her reply was fast, her gaze almost shy.

"I like it here first thing. It's quiet. Maybe I'm just addicted to the coffee." She scribbled something in her book, then punched the keys of the calculator. "Maybe you are."

"Or maybe it's the company?" he said, watching to see how she would react to that.

She looked up briefly. "Could be." She closed the book and pushed the calculator away. "Let me get you set up for the day," she said, walking past him and towards the café area.

He waited as she got to work.

"Cinnamon bun, or low-calorie muffin?" she asked.

"You know me."

She picked out a cinnamon bun using the serving tongs.

"Does any of that low-calorie stuff sell?"

"Like hotcakes," she replied "Moms, new moms especially, love them. To have here or to go?"

He would have liked to sit here, but he sensed she had things to prepare and him hanging around would only get in her way. "To go, please."

"And latte?"

"And latte." Now to tell her. "I've decided to have a thirtieth birthday party."

"You have?"

"Shelly twisted my arm. Says I've been in denial."

"We discussed your denial," Leigh replied.

"She told me."

"But good for you, about the party. I think everyone should celebrate their birthday, especially these big milestone birthdays."

"Yeah?" he asked, curious. "What about you?"

She looked at him as if he was asking a silly question. "I haven't turned thirty yet," she reminded him. "I'm the same age as Shelly, remember."

"So you are." He geared up for it. "How could I forget? I suppose Hank will organize something for you, maybe even whisk you away somewhere nice."

"I guess he will."

She hadn't even blinked an eye. Cool as a cucumber, keeping up the pretense.

"I want you to bake my cake."

"What?" She laughed, it was a nervous type of laugh, but she looked genuinely surprised.

"The birthday cake for my party. I would like you to make it."

"But I... I don't bake."

"You do!"

"I only bake a few things for the bookshop. I don't bake all of them. Most of those big fancy cakes are store-bought."

If she was hoping to change his mind, it wasn't going to work.

"You're being serious," she said, when he didn't reply.

"I am being serious."

"Rourke," she said, shaking her head. "I'm not a baker. I couldn't do justice to a thirtieth birthday cake."

"I don't want a big fancy cake with a bunch of fancy decoration. Something nice and simple, but delicious."

"You can get something nice and delicious and that looks like a decent birthday cake from a proper cake shop."

It came to him the moment he said it. "Like your lemon drizzle loaves. Just bake me a cake like that. A bigger version, enough for thirty people. That's all I want. You don't even need to ice it."

"You really want me to bake it?"

"I wouldn't ask otherwise. I'll pay you for it, of course."

She brushed a lock of hair away from her face. "I won't take any money from you for it."

"That's not right." He wasn't going to let her do this for nothing. "I'd like you to bake it, and I want to pay you, and of course, you're invited to help me celebrate. Shelly will be there as well, so you can both catch up all over again."

She stared back at him, not looking too enthused by the invite. But he understood why now.

"You don't have to invite me, Rourke." The slight shrug of her shoulders said more than words would have. But he was going to explain it to her anyway. "I know you think we're not friends, Leigh. That you think we don't usually mix in the same circles socially, and that you're Shelly's friend, but, it's no big deal, right? We're not in school anymore."

"I'll bake your cake."

"Thank you. I was hoping you'd say that."

CHAPTER 23

"He wants me to bake him a cake."

Mackenzie was getting ready to close up the shop. She turned around. "Who?"

"Rourke."

"You finally plucked up the courage to face him?"

"He showed up just as I'd opened, and I wasn't even open to the public yet." Her attempts at hiding from him hadn't gone too well.

"He obviously likes you," said Mackenzie, eyeing her with a mischievous smile.

"No," Leigh replied firmly. "He wanted to ask me a favor. He's having a party. Roxy's doing the catering and he wants me to bake him a cake."

"But you're not a baker."

"That's what I told him." She wasn't sure why he had asked her; it was one thing liking her cakes, but to have her bake one for a party? She'd been mulling their early morning conversation over in her mind all day and now she worried that she was becoming more paranoid, wondering if he had, somehow, figured out that she had been behind the notes.

"He must really like your cakes then," Mackenzie offered.

"He does."

Mackenzie continued to sweep the floor of her shop, then stopped. "Do you think he's figured out that it wasn't me?"

"No."

"He's a sharp guy. Observant, I'd say. You had to listen to our conversation that day, Leigh. I really didn't sound convincing."

She was reminded of Shelly's remarks about Rourke being happy, and about Shelly thinking he was interested in someone. "Do you like him?" she asked, "because it's really okay with me. I'm not in Rourke's league. I really could never hope to catch a guy like—"

"What are you talking about?" Mackenzie cried, dropping the broom handle in surprise. Had she done that on purpose or was that genuine surprise? Shelly had said Rourke had seemed happy, and seeing him earlier today, she'd noticed he'd looked more relaxed. The only thing that had changed between last week and now was that he'd heard Mackenzie confess. And if he was happy because of that, it could only mean one thing.

"Just that…if you are interested in him, you don't need to pretend or try and hide it from me."

"I'm not pretending. I'm absolutely one hundred percent not interested in that man. Why do you keep insisting on it?"

She didn't want to get into a disagreement with Mackenzie over this. They weren't best friends, not the way she and Shelly were. She hadn't known her decades long, even though she'd asked her for such a huge favor. But equally, she didn't want her friend to hold back on her attraction if she was interested in Rourke.

"Shelly said he was really happy. She seemed to think it might have been because he'd met someone."

"I can assure you it's not me." Mackenzie picked up her broom and held onto the handle with both hands. "Leigh. I don't want to keep hearing about Rourke. I don't mind hearing about you and Rourke, but there is no me and Rourke, so, please, don't keep thinking there is."

"I'm sorry," she wiped her hand over her forehead. "This has been a difficult few days."

Mackenzie put her broom away and walked over to her. "Maybe you need to own up to your feelings for Rourke, instead of hiding behind them?"

"I don't."

"You don't?" Mackenzie quizzed.

Leigh was about to say that she didn't have any feelings for Rourke, but she would only be lying. Caught up in the silliness of the love notes mess, she now found herself second-guessing everything he said, and making every step he took to mean something. Like his early morning appearance at the bookshop recently.

"I don't have any feelings for him," she said, finding an inner strength from somewhere. "He's asked me to bake his cake, so I guess I'm going to end up baking his cake."

"I hope he's inviting you to the party."

"He is."

"And I hope you're going to go."

"I am. I have to drop the cake off."

Mackenzie looked at her knowingly. "All right then."

The next few weeks passed quickly. She wasn't sure if she was getting things out of perspective or not, but Rourke seemed to spend more time at the bookshop than ever before. He sometimes brought his work in with him in the afternoon, and sat in the corner working away for a couple of hours. When she'd asked him about it once, he'd claimed that he liked a change of scenery, and that he liked the smell of freshly baked cakes, and the ambiance in the bookshop, and as long as his boss didn't fire him for it, he'd continue doing it.

He wasn't the only one who had praised her on the shop. People did that all the time. It was this praise that Hank had found difficult to deal with. He'd often tell her that she'd made a mistake, that it was only a matter of time before her business collapsed. They weren't even together for that long, and he'd never been around in the early days, and yet he seemed to think he knew enough to make a judgement. When she tried to tell him that she'd managed to make a success of it around the third year, that her projections were looking good going forward, he hadn't liked hearing that one bit.

It seemed that any story about her being a success was hard for him to take.

It was on a lazy, sunny Friday afternoon that her ex walked into the bookshop again. Her nerves prickled as soon as she set eyes on him, and then she relaxed, seeing a woman with him. She really did exist, then. That was her first thought. Good luck to her, was her next thought. Leigh watched from the safety of the book service counter, and prayed that Hank and his new lady friend would go over to the café area.

She saw Rourke sitting at one of the tables there. This could get tricky if she wasn't careful. Maybe it would be better for her to disappear upstairs for a while. She moved towards the stairs, but just as she was about to go upstairs, Hank caught up with her. "Where do you think you're going?" he asked, reaching for her hand which she'd placed on the handrail.

Her stomach crawled with nerves when he stood near her. "Upstairs," she replied, moving her hand away. "Who's your friend?"

"You jealous?" he asked.

"No, Hank. I am not. I was making polite conversation." She glanced at the woman who hovered around one of the book stands and wondered if this man was subjecting her to the same withering slurs.

"Come on over and say hi to my new girlfriend."

"I'm sorting out the bookshelves upstairs."

He gave her his usual condescending stare. "The bookshelves ain't going nowhere. You scared to meet her?"

While she didn't want to do as he asked, she didn't want a scene, and therefore it would be sensible to do acquiesce.

"This is Della," he said.

"Hi," said Leigh, examining the woman's face carefully, looking for signs. She found them too; the timid look, the nervousness in the slight bob of her head.

"Nice to meet you," the woman replied, her voice timid. Leigh shivered at the reminder of those days with Hank.

"Can we get some cake and coffee?" Hank asked her.

"Go on over," Leigh replied, keeping her cool. "I've got staff now," she attempted a smile. "I don't have to do everything myself anymore."

"Aw, come on now, Leigh. Be nice. It's the first time I've brought Della here. Ain't that right, Della?"

As instructed, his girlfriend agreed. "He's told me a lot about you and your bookshop."

"Has he now?" Leigh asked, and threw Hank a cold look. She was free now. Free to believe that anything was possible, and free to breathe now that she didn't have this man stamping down on her hopes and dreams with his heaviness.

"Yeah, I have. Now are you going to give us some coffee and cake or are you going to stand here gossiping all day long?"

She didn't like his tone, and she didn't like him being in her shop. "I'm not gossiping, Hank. I'm doing my best to be polite."

"Then be polite, darling, and show us some of that service you keep harping on about."

She didn't like her ex being here, and though she didn't care that he had a new girlfriend, she had to be careful not to cause a scene. Hank didn't need much to set him over the edge.

"Oh, hey," said Rourke, suddenly appearing among them. He looked at Hank directly. "You look familiar, have we met before?" Leigh's heart plunged south. What was Rourke doing?

A silence punched the air for an awkward moment. Hank stared back, his expression hard as flint. "Not sure. Who the hell are you?" His voice was almost a snarl.

Not wanting any drama, Leigh was forced to introduce the two men.

"Ah, so *you're* Hank," replied Rourke, looking surprised. She knew he would have questions for her later.

"Do I know you?" he growled, obviously growing irritated with Rourke. "I've seen you somewhere."

"It might have been here. This is my favorite place to hang out in," Rourke replied, good-naturedly, making Leigh wish the floor would split open and suck her in. The awkwardness of the situation was beginning to weigh her down because her ex and Rourke talking as if they were best buddies wasn't going to end well.

"This is my girlfriend, Della," said Hank, the emphasis heavy on *girlfriend.* Leigh ground down on her teeth, wondering why the heck Hank was doing introducing Della? As if Rourke cared.

She was just about to leave and head towards the serving station, hoping that Hank and his new woman would follow, when Hank said to Rourke, "You look kinda familiar. Where do you work?"

"At Dyson Realty. But I've seen you here before," Rourke stated, glancing at Leigh for good measure. She knew what he was referring to. Knew that he had worked it out, that rude customer, the man being nasty to her about the Doctor Zhivago book, had been Hank, and she had left that fact out of the conversation with Rourke after. She had lied about her and Hank, and he knew it.

"Sell houses, do you?"

"That's right. Got lots of million-dollar properties in Forest Heights if you're looking."

Hank's face hardened, making Leigh more uncomfortable than ever. Rourke didn't understand this man, and he didn't know that he was riling him up. She needed to put a stop to this fast.

"We've got some muffins—" she started to say, but Hank interrupted.

"Million dollars?" Hank sniffed.

"Yeah. You interested?"

Don't, she thought, wanting to zip-lock Rourke's lips.

"In fact," said Rourke, shoving his hands into his pants pockets, and looking completely at ease, "we looked at a few properties, didn't we?" he asked, turning to Leigh. A knot twisted and sank in her gut. She didn't dare to look at the expression on Hank's face. "For a friend," she murmured weakly.

It didn't make any sense, but she couldn't think of a way to stop these two men from having some sort of underhanded competition. Then Rourke reached for her wrist. She would have pulled it away had cold shock not paralyzed her. "By the way, I've made the dinner reservation for eight."

Her mouth suddenly turned dry. She blinked. "Dinner reservation?" What was he playing at now?

"Mackenzie was supposed to let you know about the time change. Didn't she tell you?" Rourke asked.

She opened her mouth and looked at him in shock. "No." She could feel the hate roll off Hank. Could feel the tightness in him without even looking. He wouldn't like this. Even though she was no longer with him, she knew this was going to cause trouble for her.

"Let me change it to seven. Angelo and Daisy can come at

any time but I wasn't sure if you needed more time to close up the bookshop." He turned to Hank. "It's not easy trying to get a bunch of friends together for dinner, especially midweek."

Leigh couldn't believe what she was hearing. She moved her wrist away from Rourke's grasp. "Come on over and check out our cake selection," she said to Della and turned to go.

She heard Della say something to Hank about her wanting to look at some books. "Just sit down and have your cake," he snapped back at her. Leigh shivered. He hadn't changed at all.

People never did. That was the problem. But they could, with determination, learn to fight back and stand up for themselves, as she had.

She walked towards the counter and told one of the assistants to 'take care of these fine people.'

"Where are you going?" Hank asked, as she excused herself. The impertinence of the man was grating on her frazzled nerves. "I've got things to do. Don't you worry, Hank. You'll get served."

As she expected, he didn't like that she wasn't doing as he'd asked. But this was her shop, her business, and she was in charge. She walked away, and strode up the stairs, needing get away.

Rourke hadn't helped things one bit. She wondered if he'd done this because he'd caught her red-handed in her lie about her and Hank.

CHAPTER 24

*L*eigh looked as if she couldn't wait to get away from her ex, and knowing what his sister had told him, Rourke now understood why.

She was uneasy, even though she had put on a brave front.

He had finished his work and had been about to return to the office but he decided to stick around. Even though she was upstairs, and Hank and his woman were sitting only a few tables away, he didn't want to leave the bookshop while Hank was here. So he had pretended to look busy, but he was actually people-watching under the guise of working.

Every now and then he would lift his head and check to see that Hank was still sitting at his table. He didn't put it past that man to sneak upstairs and go to Leigh.

It had never been his intention to tell Leigh that he knew about her and Hank, but the situation had now been forced upon him. He had to say something. He was sure she'd be expecting him to.

A short while later, when Hank and his girlfriend left, Leigh came downstairs. She'd waited until the coast was clear, but something in her expression tightened when she looked at him.

He was on a call with a potential house buyer, but he paused for a moment, mid-call, in surprise.

By the time he had finished his call, she had already gone back upstairs. He followed her, wanting to know what he'd done wrong, because clearly he had done something. She was putting books onto a shelf.

"Hey," he said, tapping her on the shoulder gently. "Do you want to talk about it?" She didn't turn around, but stopped shelving.

"A whole heap of stuff happened just now. I have questions, but I'm not going to push."

She still didn't say anything.

"You're angry with me. I can see it. At least tell me why?"

She finally faced him. "Why did you say that we were going to a restaurant for a meal?" This shocked him, because of all the things he had expected her to be angry about, it hadn't been this.

"Why did you pretend that you and Hank were still together?" he asked.

"I never said we were together."

Oh, she was playing that game, was she? He tried to recall their past conversations. "But you never said you'd split up."

Her eyes met his and locked in one angry moment. This was fragile territory. He knew why she'd fabricated the make-believe story that she and Hank were still together, because it had worked. He hadn't, for one moment, ever considered Leigh to have been the one who'd sent the love notes.

"I didn't see why you needed to know."

"You're right. It's no business of mine," he replied calmly.

"Then why lie about the dinner reservation, and why pretend that you and I had been looking for properties in Forest Heights?"

"He came in showing off his girlfriend to you. I had to think of something to say."

"And this was what you came up with? You should write fiction for a living, Rourke, not sell properties."

He took the low punch calmly. "I was trying to protect you."

"Protect me? From what?"

He had to be careful not to give anything away. "I didn't know that was Hank, until now. That rude customer who came here a few weeks ago, the one who was giving you a hard time, you never said it was Hank."

"I want to forget that man," she said, slowly. "And I don't need to tell you everything." Guarded and holding back, she wasn't giving him an inch. He was only trying to reach in, except that Leigh wasn't someone at the bar; she wasn't a flirty, overconfident woman who was going to look at him and welcome his moves.

This was Leigh.

His sister's best friend, a woman he'd never considered in a romantic way before, but whom he had come to rely on without even knowing. A woman whose opinion he sought out without thinking. A woman he had shared things he hadn't even shared with his friends yet, because, at some deep primal level, he trusted her.

And now he wanted to get to know her but she wasn't giving him a chance to. "He wasn't nice, talking to you the way he did. Demanding that you serve him. He looked to be giving you a hard time, Leigh. How could I sit back and do nothing?"

"I get difficult customers occasionally, Rourke. I have to take care of them myself. Why are you so interested in him all of a sudden?"

"I'm not. He seemed to make you uncomfortable. I came over to make sure you were okay."

"But why pretend that you and I were together?" she asked, her expression so blank that he'd doubt himself about the poems if her name hadn't been emblazoned across them cryptically.

He hadn't. That was why he'd mentioned the others, but her question made him stop and look deeper. "Are you scared of him?"

"No."

He wasn't sure he believed her.

"It was meant to sound like a dinner with friends. Look, I stepped in because I didn't like the way he treated you."

"Not your place to."

"I beg to differ. And I still don't understand why you lied about you and him still being together." He wanted to see what she would say about it, but she looked away and was silent. He was tempted to reach out and touch her face, to make her face him, but he refrained from doing so. "You can tell me," he said, hoping to coax an admission out of her, but also, because he wanted to know how she'd ever come to date a man like that.

"There's nothing to tell." She turned towards him again.

"I made a sale," he told her, not wanting to leave her in an angry mood. "I sold a property over at Forest Heights."

"Congratulations."

"I completed the deal right here in your shop."

"In that case you deserve a slice of cake, on the house."

"Leigh," he said, trying to reach in. She was like a stone, hard and impenetrable. "Why are you so annoyed? Is it Hank? Are you angry at Hank but taking it out on me?" He was going to put it out there, test her reaction.

"You didn't need to say all that stuff. You didn't need to pretend."

"I'm sorry. I didn't know it would annoy you so much. Let me make it up to you. We could still go out for dinner. I could make good on that dinner reservation."

She looked surprised. "Was that real? The dinner with your work friends?"

"No."

She choked out a small gasp. It made him wonder why the surprise was so great. "It's only dinner, Leigh." He shrugged, then raked a hand through his hair. "I was going to meet up with my other friends but, since I made the deal here, maybe we could celebrate tonight instead, you and me, an apology dinner, if it makes you feel better." The thought of spending an evening talking to Leigh, without any interruption, without her getting up to tend to customers, or opening boxes full of books, suddenly appealed.

It was just going to be dinner, like he'd had with Shelly. There was nothing to it, no hidden intentions, but she might open up to him about that ex of hers. He wanted to know more, wanted to find out what had happened, and how come such a lovely person could end up with a loser like that. He didn't like the look of that guy. Couldn't see what in the world had possessed Leigh to ever want to go out with someone like him. "Celebrate with me," he said in a last-ditch effort to convince her.

"It's nice of you but…I was going to meet up with Mackenzie tonight."

"You've got a better offer," he said. "That's okay, maybe another time then."

"Do you want me to pass on any message to her?"

He shook his head. "It was sweet and all, Mackenzie doing that stuff," but he had nothing to say, no message to give. "I need to get back to the office. Dyson will be wondering if I've upped and left the firm."

CHAPTER 25

"Hank showed up." Leigh went over to Bloom after closing up earlier than usual. Her friend was going over some paperwork.

"Oh," said Mackenzie putting down her calculator. "How was it?"

"He has a new girlfriend. He came to show her off. I suppose he wanted to prove that he was still desirable and could easily get someone." *Poor woman.* It was her that Leigh felt most sorry for.

Mackenzie wrinkled her nose in disgust. "That's a nasty thing to do."

Not so nasty, Leigh thought. "And Rourke pretended that he and I were together."

"He did what? How?"

Leigh explained what had happened.

"Like a knight in shining armor he came to your rescue," said Mackenzie.

"Does that sound like a rescue to you, because it doesn't to me." She was scared that he might have made things worse.

"He could have just sat there and ignored it all, if he didn't care about you," Mackenzie suggested.

"He's Shelly's older brother. He knows me and has always looked out for me."

"That was pretty good of him to come over," Mackenzie insisted. "He's a good guy, Leigh."

"I know he is."

"He's being nice to you, and he flew to your defense, and you two have always been friends. And…you like him…"

"He was my go-to happy place," she said. He made her smile on the days she plastered the smile on her face just to make it through the day, so that her staff and customers could see the cheerful Leigh.

"But you like him."

"As a friend," she replied, pursing her lips together. She didn't like the way Mackenzie always threw that into the conversation, repeating it as a mantra in case it slipped Leigh's mind. Yes, she liked him, but No, she could never have him. She was fast beginning to regret ever telling Mackenzie about the notes. The girl was never going to let her forget it.

"Can't you find it in your heart to confide in him, Leigh?"

It got her thinking. Maybe she could open up to him a little, at least tell him the truth about Hank, for that news must have come as a shock to Rourke.

It had been a shock to her, to see Hank this afternoon. He'd been different, more abrasive than usual, and his snarkiness went beyond his reaction to Rourke. Not that Rourke had exactly helped the situation.

But even though she and Hank were no longer together, Hank had been abrupt with Leigh, as if he still believed he had a hold over her.

She hadn't liked that at all.

She had started to pick up the pieces of her fragile self-esteem, the ones that Hank had broken piece-by-piece. These days she felt stronger, felt freer and independent, but the fact that he could still walk into her shop and make her feel as if she wasn't good enough, that he could bully her like before and make her feel so small, prickled at her conscience.

Mackenzie was right. Rourke had been good to interject when he had. She'd been angry with Hank and the way he had treated her. She was doing her best to move on from that situation, but she clearly had a way to go. She'd taken her anger for Hank and turned it on Rourke. It wasn't right. She wasn't angry with him. He'd done a nice thing for her by pretending that he'd booked a dinner reservation, and instead of thanking him for coming to her rescue, she'd ended up being miserable towards him.

On top of that she had lied to him about her and Hank being together.

She had to make it up to him. An apology or something. Or the truth about her and Hank.

That would be a start.

CHAPTER 26

"What are we celebrating now?" Reed asked, finally turning up almost an hour late. Rourke lifted his beer bottle for a toast.

"He's discovered who his secret admirer is," replied Dylan, winking. Even though there was no way his friend could know this, and Rourke was sure he was joking, he still marveled at the man's capacity to pick up on these vibes. "That stuff isn't on my radar anymore," he replied, lying easily. "We, my friends, are celebrating another beautiful commission check." He clinked his bottle with theirs. "Sold another condo over at Forest Heights."

"And the secret admirer?" Dylan asked, "What's the latest on that? You must have some idea, not to mention enough letters for a book of love poems by now."

Rourke shook his head. "I told you, they stopped a while back. Haven't had another one since." He wasn't ready to tell them anymore.

"Those places at the Heights sure are selling like hotcakes," said Reed, thankfully bringing the conversation back to easier matters. Rourke took a swig from the bottle then set it on the table. "This was one of the larger condos. It went for a cool million dollars."

Dylan whistled. "A million?"

"Merry's place would have been around that much," said Rourke, surprised that Dylan had no idea. After all, Dylan's girlfriend had recently bought a place there. "How's Merry settling in?"

"She's loving it," Dylan replied.

"Hard not to," said Rourke. The luxury development overlooked a lake and was on the edge of the woods. It was a beautiful place to live, and even more beautiful for the likes of him who gained so much from selling the properties there.

"I really need to start working on more developments like that," mused Reed,

Dylan blinked a couple of times before saying, "As if you need any more money."

"Leave some for us," Rourke complained. Some men had all the luck, and Reed Knight had plenty of luck and money.

"If I make money, you make money," Reed countered. "That's why we're here, isn't it, to celebrate your latest deal?"

"Yeah." It was good meeting his friends for a beer, but he would have liked it if Leigh hadn't turned him down and the two of them had gone out for a bite to eat instead.

"Stop trying to change the subject," Dylan persisted. "Tell us about the love letters." The guy could be like a bulldog when it came to some things, and Rourke could tell that he wasn't going to let this go.

"They're not love letters. They're just poems. Lines of verse." He tried to make a joke out of it. "Seriously, guys. Who does that these days, right?"

"Someone romantic, someone old-fashioned," replied Dylan.

"Someone who doesn't want to be found out," offered Reed.

"Someone you might have pissed off and who's trying to make you think you have an admirer."

He chuckled. This was sweet, listening to their reactions and their logic. If he hadn't already figured out who it was, he might have started to take their suggestions seriously. "Thanks," he said instead. "Great insight, guys."

"Were they sexy, these poems?" Reed asked.

"No."

"Romantic?" Dylan asked.

He shrugged. "Maybe."

"Give us an example," Reed begged.

"Uh…" He scratched his head, partly not wanting to reveal anything from them, and partly feeling a little silly. He wished he hadn't said a word at all now, but three beers later and his tongue had loosened. "Something like, being lost and not found."

"Being lost and not found?" Reed parroted.

Rourke clamped his mouth shut.

"What else?" Dylan asked.

He wasn't sure he was going to give them another line. "I can't remember."

"I bet he's lying," Reed said to Dylan.

"I'm just glad he told us," Dylan replied. "Even if it was four love letters later."

He wasn't going to mention that he'd received a fifth. "They're not love letters," he shot back.

"They sound kind of lovey-dovey to me." Reed held his gaze as the two men stared at one another. "Surely you must have a clue by now?"

"No idea," he lied. "And I'm not bothered," he said, repeating himself. "It's no big deal."

Reed chortled. "One month on, and you're telling us you've received no more cards, and you have no clue, and you don't care. You seriously expect us to believe that?"

"Oh," he should have seen this one coming. "Why don't you two clever guys come up with useful suggestions then, if you must insist on going on about them?"

"For Starling Bay's Casanova? It could be anyone," replied Reed, laughing as he lifted his bottle to his lips.

"You're right there," said Dylan, clinking his bottle against Reed's. They laughed in unison.

"Thanks for the suggestions," Rourke stated, his voice heavy with sarcasm.

"Don't be like that." Dylan put down his bottle and tried to look more serious. "Who do you think it could be? You must have some idea."

He was going to enjoy playing this game. "I thought it might be Shay at one time."

"You said that last time, and then you said you didn't think it was her."

"Want me to ask Jenna for you?" Reed offered.

"No," he replied hastily. He didn't want anyone doing any investigative work on his behalf, since there was no further investigation to be done. "Don't ask her. I still don't think it's her."

He was having fun pretending he had no clue, but equally, he was getting frustrated about how to broach Leigh. He had to work on getting her to open up, and to confide in him, and right now he didn't know if her baking him a cake and coming to his party was going to help do it. But a guy could hope.

"Oh…" said Dylan, drawing out the vowel. "Then who is it?"

"I don't know."

"You sounded certain just then, as if you already knew who it was."

"I thought it might be Roxy," he said, throwing Mr. FBI a bone. "We double-dated once so it's not entirely impossible."

"Roxy?" asked Dylan, sounding as if he didn't quite agree.

"But you've dated most of the eligible women in Starling Bay," Reed countered with a grin. "We could be looking at a large sample of women to draw from."

"You two make it sound as if I'm the only playboy in town."

"Aren't you?" they both asked at the same time.

He shook his head. Maybe this was what Leigh thought of him. He paused, thinking of all the times in the past he'd told her about his dates and how he had wined and dined them. It was one thing his friends having this opinion of him, but someone like Leigh? Someone sweet, and caring, and kind and… and someone he was starting to care about. "Knock it off, guys," he said, forcing a smile.

"Does he seem fragile to you?" he heard Reed ask.

Then Dylan replied, "He's been touchy for weeks."

"Think he's growing up at last?" was Reed's next question.

"Ha ha," Rourke replied. "I'm dying with laughter here." He had a way to go in order to win Leigh's trust. He could see that now. "Speaking of growing up, make sure you show up on time at my party," he said. "I don't want either of you turning up two hours late." He looked at Reed in particular. His friend had a reputation for getting too wrapped up in his business matters, even on weekends, and had been late on many occasions.

"I wouldn't be late for your party," Reed assured him. "It's the first party Jenna's been invited to with my friends." He cleared his throat, "Obviously she was at the Valentine's Day ball, but she was working that night."

Rourke remembered. So she had been.

"That's why she's slightly nervous. She's not sure if people still believe Olivia, and all that stuff she implied."

"That's old news," said Dylan.

"People have forgotten, and you shredded Olivia's reputation, pal, so people will see she lied," Rourke told him.

"Merry and I will be there," said Dylan. "Merry's good at

making people feel at ease. Jenna will be fine. Who are you bringing?" Dylan asked him.

"Nobody."

"You don't have a date?" Reed asked, exaggerating his shock at this news.

Rourke's jaw stiffened. "I haven't dated in months," he replied smoothly. "You were too busy with Jenna to notice."

"Funny," Reed replied.

"But true," he said, pointing a finger at his friend.

"Please tell me you're not inviting Hyacinth," Dylan said.

Rourke chortled. "Want me to, pal?" Hyacinth was a prominent person in Starling Bay, and a self-proclaimed busybody. She was also, at a guess, much older than his parents. "No way. My parents aren't even invited. Shelly's coming though."

"Awesome," replied Reed.

"Looking forward to it?" Dylan asked.

He sighed and nodded. "Yeah, strangely enough, I am." It was also, he had decided, the night he was going to let Leigh know that he knew her secret.

CHAPTER 27

He'd invited Mackenzie to his party a few weeks ago, but he hadn't yet given out a formal invite. And though he didn't want to admit to it, he'd been avoiding the florist as much as possible. It was awkward. She'd obviously been primed into making the admission, but he knew she hadn't sent the notes. Any encounter was bound to be forced, but he needed to make good on the invite.

And he needed to buy a bouquet of flowers.

"Hey," said Mackenzie as soon as he walked in.

"Hey there. I've been meaning to give you this for a while," he said, not wanting to waste any time. He pulled out a small invite he'd done a few nights ago. Talk about last minute. It was a small card with his address and the time and date of the party. "I guess I should have handed these out when I told people about the party. I haven't been that organized."

"Thank you. I will be there. A thirtieth party. Wow! That's a big milestone."

"It's not a big party or anything," he said, wanting to lower her expectations. He hadn't wanted this event, but now he needed to step things up a little, judging from how many questions he'd already had from everyone he'd invited.

No way was it going to be a fancy dress, which had been Angelo's suggestions, or an affair like Reed's Valentine's Day ball. Though he knew Reed hadn't been too keen about that either. That ball had purely been Olivia's baby. In any case, he didn't have the room to have that type of event, nor the huge guest list, or a budget the size of Alaska.

Nor did he want that type of party. But he had music, and food, and a good variety of friends, even if Shelly had been on his case the last two weeks to get everything done.

"Leigh told me she's baking a cake for you."

"I have a thing for her lemon drizzle loaf," he admitted.

"She does make a good lemon drizzle." He cast his eyes around the shop, until his gaze settled on a bunch of lilies. Too much, he thought. Too show-offy. Then he saw bunches of roses nearby.

Again, too much.

It wasn't the cost he was worried about, but Leigh's reaction. He wondered what she would make of it if he suddenly gave her a bunch of roses. He'd given her flowers before but that had been before he knew. Somehow, not knowing had made things easier.

He walked around, examining the flowers on display, searching for something appropriate.

"I can't make up my mind," he confessed. Mackenzie walked over.

"What's the occasion?" she asked.

"No occasion." Then to call her bluff, "The roses are nice."

"Who's the special lady?"

"Leigh."

"Leigh?"

He could almost see the cogs in her brain turning. "To cheer her up," he explained. "Her ex came to the bookshop yesterday. I don't think Leigh liked him being around."

"She mentioned that you stepped in."

"She was annoyed I stepped in."

"It was sweet of you."

"She didn't see it that way."

"That's the thing about Leigh," said Mackenzie, folding her arms. "She sometimes can't see what's right under her nose."

"You think so?"

"I really do think so." Mackenzie looked at him for a moment longer, and he wasn't sure if she was trying to figure him out, to determine whether he might have guessed. Buying Leigh flowers might have tipped her off. Heck, what did it matter now? He was going to confront Leigh at the party anyway. And then, just like that, he decided to come clean. "It wasn't you, was it?"

"What do you mean?" She tilted her head slightly.

"Those poems. I know it wasn't you."

If she was surprised by his question, she was doing a great job of hiding it. Her mouth opened. "I…"

"You don't have to lie about it anymore, Mackenzie. It was sweet of you to cover for her."

"For who?"

"You know full well who. For Leigh."

She blinked in surprised. "How did you—"

"It wasn't hard for me to see what was under my nose."

A thin smile formed on her face. She let out a loud sigh. "Clever man. I'm so glad you figured it out. I hated lying about it."

"I could tell it was painful for you to make that confession."

She grinned again, and looked as if a huge weight had been lifted from her shoulders. "I told her to 'fess up, but she wouldn't listen."

Leigh was strong minded. He could see that about her. She had a soft exterior, but she was made of steel underneath. Running a business was hard work. It took blood and guts, and taking on the kind of risk she had, opening a café in one corner of the shop, had required serious backbone. Leigh had expanded and refurbished and worked hard to get where she was. That took nerves of steel. On top of it all, she'd put up with a monster like Hank. While he couldn't understand what she'd ever seen in that scumbag, the fact remained, she'd come out of it and somehow still managed to put on a smile, and exude a positive attitude daily. She opened that bookshop just so that customers and others like him could come and relax and enjoy her lemon drizzle loaves and cups of coffee. "Don't tell her I know. I'll tell her, but I want to do it when the time is right."

"I won't say a word."

He picked up a bunch of colorful peonies. "Do these work?" he asked. "Do they say *I care* without coming over too strong?"

"They do, and they're pretty," she commented, wrapping them up for him.

"Wish me luck."

"You don't need luck, Rourke. She was the one sending those notes, remember. You already know how she feels. She just needs to know that you know she exists."

"I do know she exists."

"Do you?"

"Yes."

"Do you see her, as in *really* see her?"

What was Mackenzie talking about? "Of course I do."

"Then did you guess straightaway that it was her?"

He hadn't. "She had a boyfriend, or she pretended she did."

Mackenzie lifted her chin and stared down at him. "I'll give you that, but even if she hadn't had a boyfriend, would you have ever considered it could be her?"

She had him there. "No, because…because she's my little sister's friend."

"So you don't really know she exists?"

He understood. "I'll keep that in mind," he replied.

"Thanks for the invite."

He went directly to the bookshop after, and found Leigh at the book counter. He waited for her to finish serving a customer.

"For you," he said, stepping forward with the bunch of flowers.

It might have been wishful thinking on his part, but he was sure her face lit up in a smile that reached her eyes. "You're going to have to stop buying me flowers all the time," she said, taking them and holding them to her nose.

"All the time? Hardly."

"This is the second time."

"Are you complaining? Because most women wouldn't complain if a guy brought them flowers."

She laughed. "I'm not complaining. They're beautiful, thank you. But what's the occasion?"

"It's an apology," he said, pleased to see this reaction from her. "I'm sorry about yesterday, for hijacking that scenario with your ex."

Her smile suddenly lost some of its warmth. "You didn't need to buy me flowers, and you don't need to apologize for that."

"I do. It was wrong of me to suggest about the meal and to pretend that we'd seen some properties together. Of course it sent out the wrong message, but he was parading his newest girlfriend. I didn't want you to feel bad."

"I didn't feel bad. Trust me on that. He's not a nice man."

It was rare, and unexpected, this sudden revelation from her. "No?" He'd sensed it anyway, but he wanted her to tell him.

Her brow furrowed. "I'm sorry I was so ungrateful to you. You were only standing up for me."

"You looked uneasy. I couldn't look away."

"I wasn't angry at you. I was angry at him, and I took it out on you."

"Angry at him for what, Leigh?"

She hesitated, and her brows pushed together, like they always did when she was busy concentrating on something. "I was angry at myself for letting Hank come here and make me feel so small."

"Is that how he makes you feel?"

She gave a small nod, but her lips were tightly closed, as if she was trying to hold her composure. She didn't even look at him.

"I might be selfish saying this, but I can't see you being with someone like that."

"Selfish?"

"You deserve to be treated better, Leigh. You deserve so much more."

Her gaze shot up to his face. "You can't tell that from how he looks."

"I'm not talking about how he looks." The man hadn't exactly looked rough, but it was his whole manner. He seemed abrasive even before he'd opened his mouth. "I'm talking about how he spoke to you, how he treated you. You don't deserve that. Nobody does."

She looked suddenly fragile, as if she was going to fall apart if he questioned her further, so he didn't. "I only wanted to cheer you up with the flowers."

She cleared her throat. "It was very thoughtful of you."

They stared at one another for the briefest of seconds, and he was almost tempted to tell her now. Tell her that he knew so that they could move on. But move on to where? Mackenzie's words floated back to him. *You already know how she feels.*

But Leigh wasn't easy to pry open, and if he moved too fast, she might retreat. This was new territory for him, and he wasn't quite sure how to navigate these waters. Usually, his laser vision allowed him to target a beautiful woman then entice her into a conversation with a drink, or a wink, or a smile, or a line.

Leigh was so much harder, and at the same time, so much softer.

Timing.

It was all about timing, and right now wasn't the right time.

"Shelly's so excited about your party."

"I know. My sister's been bugging me to make sure everything is ready. Are you all set with the cake?" he asked, shaking his head. "I didn't think it through properly, asking you to bake my cake even though you're running your business and probably have no free time on your hands."

She smiled. "It's just a cake, Rourke. A big cake, but nothing that I can't handle. I see it as an honor, actually."

"You're honored to bake my cake?"

"Sure I am. I just hope I can do it justice."

"I have every faith in you."

"I was planning to veer off the recipe slightly. Would that be a problem?"

That warmed his heart. "No, not at all. Do whatever you want. Anything you bake is great."

"I was going to decorate it with a simple frosting. I know you're counting your calories—not that you need to—" she said quickly, "But you can't have a plain old birthday cake."

"I'm happy with whatever you decide. Shelly says she's going to give you a lift to my place on the day."

"I'll need to hold the cake, so she's offered to drive me there."

"But if you want, I could come by and pick you up instead." That way, he could tell her he knew of her secret before the party started. "Shelly will probably spend hours getting ready, you know what she's like."

"But it's your party! You can't be my taxi-driver."

"I don't see it as being your taxi-driver. You're making my cake, Leigh. It's the least I can do."

"That's very sweet of you, but I can't have you pick me up on the evening of your party. Shelly's coming, and besides, I want to surprise you with the cake."

Any other woman would have jumped at the chance. Not Leigh. It wasn't that she was playing hard to get. She wasn't even in the game. He recalled Mackenzie's words. *She just needs to know that you know she exists.* "I look forward to seeing your work of art," he told her.

"I'm not sure it will be a work of art, but I hope you'll like it."

He already knew he would.

CHAPTER 28

*E*dible flowers. Was that going over the top? Leigh walked into Bloom just before Mackenzie was about to close the shop.

"I hear you got another bunch of flowers from your favorite man."

"Shhhh," Leigh hissed, then looked around as if Rourke might spring out of thin air.

"Don't worry, nobody's here," said Mackenzie, teasing.

"He told you he was buying them for me?"

"Yes," replied Mackenzie, in a why-are-you-asking-me-that-silly-question tone. "I'm a florist, and he wanted my opinion."

"To buy flowers?"

"He didn't want to offend you."

What did that mean? "How's he going to offend me by buying me flowers?"

"He was afraid you'd get upset if he brought you something that meant something. Like roses."

"Well, it was nice of him to cheer me up," she replied, not wanting to launch into a discussion about what roses might mean.

Rourke would never buy her roses, and even if he had, she would assume he felt sorry for her.

"He's a really nice guy, Leigh. The more I get to know him, the more I am convinced of that."

She looked at her friend, wondering if Mackenzie had spilled the beans to Rourke. But instead, Mackenzie rolled her eyes. "I'm not interested in him, Leigh. But I think he's interested in you."

"I came here to ask you about edible flowers," she said, completely ignoring the comment.

"For?"

"The cake. I'm getting carried away with it."

Mackenzie hummed. "Could it be because you care?"

"He's asked me to bake the cake and I need it to look good."

"Because you care what he thinks."

"Well, yes, of course I care what he thinks. I don't want to mess it up, and you wouldn't either if someone asked you to do the same. I've been watching YouTube channels."

"For what?"

"Tips on baking the cake."

"You know how to bake a cake."

"I'm taking it a step further. I'm going to add a frosting, not make it completely a lemon drizzle, but lighter, with a hint of elderflower, then decorate it with buttercream and maybe fresh flowers. Do you think that's too much?"

The way Mackenzie was looking at her told her that she did.

"Maybe I'll ditch the fresh flowers, and just put a frosting on it." Then, "Do you sell edible flowers?"

Mackenzie looked at her for a stunned second. "No, I don't. You have to get them from a specialty shop."

"Hmmm." Leigh had thought as much.

"You're going to a lot of trouble to impress Rourke."

She folded her arms defiantly. "I am not."

"Didn't he just want one of your regular lemon drizzle loaves?"

"He did, but I can't give him an average basic cake. Not for his thirtieth. I have to make it a bit more fancy."

"Do you?"

"Yes!" Leigh could feel the heat crawling up her cheeks. She wanted Rourke to have a nice cake and didn't understand why Mackenzie was making it out to be something more than that.

"Why don't you just tell Rourke you sent those love letters?"

"They're not love letters, they're notes. And they were supposed to be a jokey fun thing."

"Except they're not a jokey, fun thing, are they?"

She ground her teeth together. "We're getting along better than ever," she declared, but wasn't sure what she meant by that. "We're friends, and everything's back to normal. I was just on a downer after Hank, and I needed a little pick-me-up. I keep telling you, that's all it was."

Except that splitting up with Hank had been the pick-me-up.

Things between her and Rourke had been good. Maybe telling Mackenzie to own up to the love notes had done the trick, but he definitely seemed less stressed out.

With him standing up for her, and him giving her flowers, listening to her, she'd felt able to trust him. It felt good telling him a little about Hank and the way he made her feel. Telling Shelly about her miserable few months with Hank was like letting a load off her soul, but confiding little things to Rourke made her heart come alive again. She couldn't explain it, the way he listened, the way his voice dropped when he wanted to know, the way he looked at her sometimes, as if he wanted to say something.

She found herself falling, found herself moving closer to him emotionally, but at the same time tried to hold back from tumbling in deeper.

Maybe Mackenzie was right, and she was getting too carried away with this task of baking his birthday cake.

"What are you wearing?" Mackenzie asked. She hadn't even thought of that, and shrugged in response. Mackenzie looked horrified. "You haven't decided what you're wearing?"

"No."

"And you're more concerned about the cake and the frosting and the edible flowers? He would love whatever you baked for him, Leigh, even if you accidentally burned it."

"Don't say that." She shivered at the thought.

"I'm kidding! Look at you. You're so stressed about his birthday cake."

Leigh rolled her eyes. "Obviously." Making someone's thirtieth birthday cake was a big deal.

"I'm coming over to your place tonight," said Mackenzie, a determined look settling over her face.

"I'm going shopping for fresh ingredients."

"It's cake, Leigh, not sushi! I'm coming over and I'm going to put together an outfit that will have Rourke eating out of your hands."

Leigh wrinkled her nose. "I'd rather he ate out of a plate."

Mackenzie huffed out a loud irritated breath. "I'm going to find you a sexy little number to wear to his party."

"I don't have a sexy number."

"Sweet petunias," murmured Mackenzie. "In that case, I'm going to have to take you shopping."

"No. Absolutely not." She was not going to have Mackenzie drag her into shops she'd never set foot in just to buy her something she probably wouldn't like, for an event at which Rourke wouldn't even notice her.

"I'll do your hair, curl it a little," said Mackenzie, cocking her head and staring at Leigh's hair. "Yes," she said, talking to herself and nodding, "A slight wave, I think. I'll blow dry it so it's got bounce, and," she walked around her as if she was a mannequin. "Heels, definitely heels. You'll have to shave your legs and underarms…"

"I do shave my legs and underarms," Leigh cried. "I'm not a Neanderthal."

"Then how come we never see them? You're always covered up, wearing full-length lumberjack shirts and yoga pants"

"They're not always yoga pants."

"They're stretch. It should be illegal for anyone under the age of fifty to wear stretch clothing."

"You're evil."

"No, honey, I'm your fairy godmother."

Exasperated, Leigh's shoulders slumped. "I should never have stepped foot in here today."

Mackenzie smiled. "You're hiding under those clothes. You need to shine."

"I'm not a window."

"You're not a cave, either."

"What's with you today?" Leigh asked.

"I just think it would be even better if you came clean, with Rourke. Tell him everything. He might surprise you."

That's what she was afraid of. Afraid that he might surprise her with a tall, leggy supermodel-like creature.

"No flowers, then," she said, deciding to leave. "Just a simple, no-frills buttercream frosting."

"I'll be at the bookshop by six, Cinders. Make sure you're ready. We're going shopping."

CHAPTER 29

"I'll be in the kitchen for most of the afternoon," she told her shop assistants. She'd warned them not to disturb her, unless there was a flood or a fire.

After a late night yesterday, what with shopping for an outfit that was Mackenzie-approved, she'd overslept. She had no time to waste because it was the day of Rourke's party and she was going to bake his cake. She had adapted it slightly, it still had the tangy lemon flavor that he loved, but it wasn't going to be shaped like a loaf. It was going to be round, like a proper birthday cake. She was going to keep the frosting simple and write on it in deep purple.

She'd been baking a variation of the cake for the past week and selling it at the bookshop. The regulars had loved it. She just hoped that Rourke would. Her fear was that he might think she had gone over the top. Or worse, he might not like the frosting, given his recent diet-mania but something told her that he would pretend to like it no matter what.

He had come in every day this past week. Lately, with them talking, and her starting to confide in him, she sometimes thought that he might have his suspicions and might have guessed that she had been behind the notes.

But if he had known, he would have avoided the bookshop, and the last thing he would have done would be to buy her flowers. She wasn't his type, she reminded herself.

Tonight would be a test of her strength, to watch him from the sidelines as he brought a special female friend along to his party. With that thought putting a downer on her mood, she got to work.

A few hours later, with two large layers of the cake baked and cooling on a wire rack, she was about to get started on the frosting.

"There's someone out here to see you," said one of her assistants, a new girl who had started a few weeks ago. Leigh was just about to mix together the icing sugar and butter. She looked up, slightly annoyed by the interruption. "Can you deal with it?"

"He said he wanted to speak to you."

This was annoying. Customers often had queries about books they had ordered.

"I told him you were busy, but he insisted."

Leigh wiped her hands with a dishcloth, and went out onto the shop floor, and stopped. It was like a punch to her face, seeing Hank on the other side of the serving counter. Her gut tightened in defense.

"You wanted to see me?"

"I want a slice of cake, and a cup of your finest coffee."

A knot of anger twisted in her throat. Who did he think he was, commanding her around like that? "I'm busy, but my assistant here will serve you." She turned to leave, not caring how rude her response had been for she had no intention of serving him.

"I'm your customer," he growled. "Ever heard of customer satisfaction?"

She turned and saw that people close by had stopped and were staring at him. Rage simmered in her belly, then mixed with fear and threw up a taste of bitter bile in her throat. "I told you that my assistant would serve you. I'm busy." She knew what this was, part of his control, part of his making sure she did what he told her to, but she wasn't going to let him win.

"I want my cake and my coffee," he said, in a voice so deadly calm and low that it scared her. Beside her, she could sense her assistant hovering, waiting, feeling afraid.

"I'll serve this gentleman. Why don't you go and clear the tables," she told her.

Hank's face turned calm, his hard expression suddenly softening at her apparent defeat. Around the shop, people continued going about their way. "That's better," he said, giving her a smile that chilled her bones.

"Which one?" she asked.

"You should know which one."

She hated this. Hated that he could come in here and make her be his puppet. "I don't know. I've forgotten. Which one?" If she picked the muffin he would say 'No', if she picked the chocolate cake he would say the same. It was all a game to him. He liked being difficult, and he'd been worse ever since the split.

"Forgotten because you have a new boyfriend?" he asked.

"The chocolate cake, isn't it?" she asked, ignoring his question and offering a half-dead smile instead. "With strong coffee, to go?" She hoped and prayed that he would say 'Yes', even though she knew it would never be that simple.

"Yes, to go. You don't think I'd want to sit in this hellhole, do you?"

She wondered why had he set foot in here if he hated it so much? She boxed up his cake slice and prepared his coffee silently, grateful to know that he would be on his way soon.

Time-wise she was doing well. She'd get Rourke's cake

finished and iced, and then rush home for a quick shower and to get ready.

She had managed to convince Mackenzie not to wait for her—more because she didn't want Mackenzie to Barbie-style her hair. She'd promised to wear the dress they'd bought, and the high-heels, and make an effort, but she wanted to get dressed herself.

She'd bought a lovely dark blue dress, after a ten-minute debate with Mackenzie about why she would never wear a bright red dress. It was slim-fitting, to the point that Mackenzie wolf-whistled when Leigh had come out of the changing room. "You have curves," she'd commented, clapping. "And boobs, and a waist. Why for the love of tulips are you hiding all your assets?"

She had to admit, the sexy high-heeled sandals gave her some height.

But even though she was going to all this effort and doing her best to transform from her everyday casual clothes to this, Rourke still wouldn't notice her.

"There you go," she said, handing over the food, and taking Hank's money. "And here's the change." She was curious to know what had happened to Della, but she didn't care. She only wanted him to leave, and when he did, without saying another word, she was speechless.

A few hours later, the cake was ready. It looked beautiful, regal almost, with its pale off-white frosting, and a 'Happy 30th Birthday, Rourke.' She'd done a twirl on it with the icing, a tip she'd picked up from an online video. Flowers would have looked stunning, but, she told herself in an attempt not to be down about it, they might not have been apt for a man's thirtieth birthday.

"Beautiful," she murmured, admiring the cake from all angles. She took a few pictures and sent them to Mackenzie and Shelly, and within seconds got emoji-filled replies back.

"Not bad for a bookshop owner," she thought, truly pleased that she had managed to make such a professional-looking cake.

She had decided to close the shop half an hour early, seeing that it usually quieted down by the end of the day on Saturday.

Leaving the kitchen, she walked over to the cash counter and told both of her assistants that they could go home early.

"If you girls can clear away the tables and the dishes, I'll turn out the lights upstairs and check all around."

Her assistants knew the ropes now, and were good at tidying up, but she still liked to do the final round and check everything herself.

Eager to close up and get home, she rushed around. The baking had left her hot and sweaty, and she needed a shower. She was also excited about getting changed into her new dress, and doing her hair up; making a proper effort, for once, and transforming herself into someone Rourke had never seen before.

She tidied up the shelves a little, then turned out the lights and came back downstairs.

The only thing left to do was to check the displays downstairs, and the cash register, which she always did at the very end, with any urgent paperwork. Only then would she be ready to go home.

As she checked along the aisles, fixing the bookshelves, straightening books that jutted out, and picking up the ones that had been placed haphazardly on the display tables, she thought she heard a noise. "Heidi? Larissa?" She called out for her shop assistants.

No answer.

They'd obviously left.

She walked towards the cash register, and then stopped. The hairs on the back of her neck stood upright like soldiers.

"That was darn good, that slice of cake."

She spun around, her heart galloping. "We're closed."

"That's not what it says on your sign." Hank stared at her, his back leaning against the glass of the cake display counter.

"I'm closing early today."

"Your sign says six o'clock."

The room suddenly started to spin around her. The shock of Hank's appearance was playing tricks on her. "I've decided to close early today." She wasn't in the mood to explain or reason with him. This was her shop, and these were her rules.

"You never closed early for me. Where are you going?" he sneered. "Somewhere with your boyfriend?"

She walked towards him, because she didn't want him to think she was scared, even if she was starting to feel it. Alone in the bookshop, with just her and him, she suddenly felt vulnerable. "He's not my boyfriend."

"You liar."

"He's not."

Hank took a step towards her. "You lying little witch."

She swallowed. "You need to leave, Hank, otherwise I'll call the police."

He laughed. "And say what?" He held his hand to his ear, as if he was on the phone, "Sorry, officer, my customer won't leave." He cackled like a madman.

Her mind spun, excuses, reasons, things she wanted to say swirled around in her head. She was in danger, and she had to think, and speak carefully, because this man was volatile, and unstable. One wrong word could turn things nasty.

"You're not thinking straight, Hank. You should go home."

"When did you start seeing him?" he asked.

"We're not together. I'm not seeing anyone."

"Why are you and him going out to dinner with friends? Why are you and him looking at properties that cost a million dollars?"

She'd known this was coming, the hate and jealousy. He had never taken the break-up well, but she had never dreamed he'd still be so cut-up about it. It was almost like an obsession, something he couldn't get over. If only Rourke hadn't intervened, hadn't tried to make things better that day. Nothing good ever came of a conversation with Hank.

"I was never good enough for you, was I?"

The muscles in her jaw clenched, and she didn't know whether to reply or stay quiet. Anything she said could set him off, and she didn't want to risk that. "You weren't always nice to me, Hank."

"I tried to be nice to you."

"You tried to tell me what to do, and you got angry when I did things my way." It had been petty, but the petty things started to accumulate over time. Petty became controlling, and the controlling got beyond the normal.

They might have gotten by, had she been the type to give in, and give up, and put up with his ways. Most men probably saw her as timid and meek, those that noticed her. Hank did too, but he hadn't been able to mold her, or control her, and had been surprised, then shocked, then angry, when she had fought back.

Yes. People underestimated her, thinking she was soft and easily to manipulate, someone who would happily put herself out for others, a helper and a good-friend. She could be, but she was more than that. She suddenly remembered.

The cake.

The party.

Rourke.

A wave of courage swept over her. She had a party to go to, and a cake to deliver, and she didn't have time for this.

"I don't want any trouble, Hank. My friends will be here soon to pick me up so I'm asking you nicely to leave."

"Liar."

She blinked in confusion. "I'm not lying. It's true. I'm finishing up early because they're coming to pick me up." She said 'they' hoping that the fear of many might deter him, but he stood where he was, only a few feet away from her, staring at her like a rabid dog.

And just like that, as if on cue, her phone started to ring. The sound rang out from the kitchen. "Told you," she said, triumphantly.

He didn't move. Didn't flinch a bit, and soon the ringing stopped.

"Is it your smooth and suited boyfriend? Is he the one who's coming to get you? That darned broker, the show-off selling those houses."

"He's a friend."

"So why'd he talk to me about them houses like I couldn't afford one?"

If only Rourke knew what a problem he had created that day. "Are you jealous?" she asked, attempting a different line of questioning, even if it was a bold and careless.

"Of him?" Hank's face creased in disgust. "I can't stand people like him who think they're better than me. You and him, you're the same. You think you're better than me, too, don't you?"

"I don't go around making people feel bad the way you do. You do that all the time. You did it to me and that's why I didn't want to be with you anymore."

The phone started ringing again and she jumped, her heart jangling with fear and worry. "I need to get that," she said, "And you need to leave before my friends get here and—"

He headed for the kitchen. She rushed after him as he flung the kitchen door wide open and charged inside. And then he stood rooted to the floor as he saw the cake on the table.

"What do we have here?" he asked, walking slowly towards it. "You made this, did you?"

She didn't answer his question but eyed her cell phone which had stopped ringing again. It lay on the table, just a few inches away from the cake.

"I said, did you make this cake?" he barked.

"Yes, I did."

"Happy thirtieth birthday, Rourke," he said, reading out the writing on the top. "You made your boyfriend's birthday cake," he sneered again, and then started to laugh. If only she could get near her phone, and grab it, she could call for help.

"We'll see about that," said Hank, standing directly behind the cake.

She saw it too late, saw his big thick hands go on either side of it, messing up the smooth finish of the icing. He lifted it high, like a trophy, just above his head.

Her breath hitched in her throat.

"Lover boy's birthday cake?" He laughed, as if she'd said something hilarious.

"Put it down, Hank. Don't be silly." Her heart swooped as if she was plunging sixty feet from a crevice.

"Oops," he snarled, then dropped it. She heard the soft smack of the cake against the hard tiled floor, and her heart thudded alongside it. "No!" she screamed. "What have you done?" Her voice, her muscles, her breathing, it all locked up, as she stared at Hank, and the splattered cake all over the floor.

It had all happened in slow motion, his ugly smile, his deathly laugh.

"Tell him I said happy birthday," he said, before stepping over the spattered cake and walking out.

CHAPTER 30

"She's not answering." Rourke was beginning to get worried. Shelly had called Leigh earlier to ask how she was doing for time and she hadn't answered.

So he'd called again just now, and she still didn't answer.

"She's probably getting ready," Shelly told him. His sister was fastening her earrings, and was dressed up as if this was her party. "Aren't you getting dressed?" she asked him.

"It's still early. What's the rush?"

His place had been a hive of activity ever since the afternoon. Roxy was coming over soon with her catering crew, and the DJ had just arrived and was setting up in the small tent he'd had erected in his back yard.

Shelly had been rushing around taking care of goodness knows what, because there wasn't anything to do. Food, music, and the birthday cake, all these things were taken care of. What else was there?

Rourke was growing increasingly anxious. His guests would start arriving in the next few hours, but he'd told Reed and Dylan to come early. He wanted Jenna to feel at ease with everyone, and figured it would be good if it was just his closest friends around for a while before everyone else arrived.

"Try her again," he urged Shelly.

"Why are you so worried? She's probably getting ready. Women take longer than you guys."

He didn't doubt that, from the length of time Shelly had been in the bathroom. But Leigh wasn't like that. She was always in her usual slacks and shirt, and he wasn't going to be too surprised if she turned up in something just as comfortable, just as casual tonight.

Question was, would he have the guts to tell her tonight? He couldn't think of a better time to get this over with. "I'll just go and pick her up," he suggested, feeling suddenly uneasy.

"You?" Shelly cried, "It's your party. You have to stay here and let your guests in. You're not even dressed, Rourke, so maybe you should start to do that? I'll go and get Leigh, and you go and get dressed."

He wasn't going to win. He wasn't. She wouldn't let him. He'd smashed Rourke's cake, and then he'd left, thinking he had won. He hadn't.

She was going to start over. Bake Rourke another cake just like this one, and she would make up for lost time by not getting changed. She kept a change of clothes here in one of the cupboards, a spare in case of accidents. She'd wear that. It wasn't a party outfit, but did it matter? Rourke wouldn't even realize.

It was the cake that mattered the most.

And Hank? She would think about him later.

Later. Later. Later. When the frayed ends of her nerves calmed down and she was back in the safety of her own home. She would decide what to do about Hank.

Later.

Not now.

Now she was busy mix-mix-mixing.

She had started to make another cake, just a normal lemon drizzle loaf, the type she sold at the bookshop and the type Rourke loved.

She hadn't had time to clean the mess up from the floor. Hadn't had much time to think about what had happened. Or Hank, and what she needed to do about him. Her calm and logical brain had taken over, and she had continued doing what needed to be done.

Just as she closed the oven door, and set the timer, she heard footsteps.

Hank?

For a glass-splintering second, fear jabbed her in the chest. The kitchen door flew open, and in walked Shelly. She breathed out a huge sigh of relief.

"What happened?" Shelly cried, looking at the floor in shock. "Your beautiful cake." Her hands flew to her face as she looked up at Leigh, the corners of her eyes crinkling in concern. "You sent pictures, and it looked beautiful. How did this happen?"

"I've made another one," said Leigh, avoiding the question.

"But what happened?" Shelly asked, stepping over the cake.

"Hank came."

"What?" Shelly snapped, her face registering disbelief.

"He was here in this kitchen."

"He did this?"

"He picked it up and dropped it."

Shelly's hand flew to her mouth. "How can you be so calm?" she asked, looking worried. She placed a hand on Leigh's arm. "You need to call the police, Leigh. Press charges. Get a restraining order. You need to do *something*. The man is crazy. Has he always been like this?"

"He's not been this bad. This is another level altogether."

"Rourke was going to come and pick you up. He got worried."

"Why?"

"Why? We called a couple of times and you didn't answer. We got worried, but now that I know what's happened, I see we had good reason to be worried." She wiped a hand over her face. "I can't believe he did this. I can't believe he did this and you're so calm."

"No good me jumping up and down," Leigh replied.

"I wish you'd have some sort of reaction. At least that would be normal."

"I had to make another cake. I started it right away. It needs another twenty-five minutes. We might be a little late but—"

"Leigh," Shelly shook her by the shoulders. "Stop this. What's the matter with you? How can you bake a cake after this? I saw the pictures you sent. Your cake was magnificent."

"I can't fall to pieces over this. It's what he would want."

Shelly stared back at her, too stunned to say anything.

"He was angry, and jealous, and Rourke had said something which riled him up."

"Rourke said something? When?"

"I don't have time to explain. Let me clear up this mess on the floor."

"I'll clear up the mess, don't you worry about that, and forget the cake. My brother was worried about you; he won't care about the cake, especially when I tell him what Hank did."

"You can't tell him. Not tonight. Not on the night of his party. I don't want to ruin things for him."

Hank had ruined her cake, and he'd ruined the day for her, because she didn't have time to go home and get dressed now, but she wasn't about to let that nasty man ruin Rourke's birthday party.

"He won't care about the cake. He'll be more worried about you." Shelly stared directly into her eyes. "You told me your ex was nasty, but you never said he was a psychopath."

"He's always had a nasty side to him. I never knew it was this bad."

"I don't know what you were doing with that man, Leigh."

"He wasn't like that when we first met. He was nice to me."

"In any case, you have to report him to the police."

"For what? For smashing a cake?"

"For threatening behavior. You have to make sure he doesn't come near you again."

"Not tonight."

"But you will have to after. Promise me you will."

"I will."

"First things first," said Shelly, taking charge. "You have to get ready."

"I can't. I don't have time."

"You can, and you do have time. The party's going to go on past midnight. It won't matter if we're a little late."

"But what about the cake?" She wasn't going to have time to make it look pretty, and it hurt, because she'd created what she hoped would be something Rourke would love, only, he was never going to see it.

"Forget the cake," Shelly groaned.

"He needs a cake. It's the only thing he asked me to make."

Shelly grabbed her by the shoulders. "This is what we're going to do. You're in shock."

"I'm not in shock."

"You're..." Shelly threw her hands up in defeat. "You're baking another cake, of course you're in shock."

"I'm doing the right thing. I'm going to clean this mess up now—"

"You're going home to get dressed."

"No, I'm not."

"It's Rourke's party. If you turn up looking as if you've just left the bookshop, he won't be too pleased."

"He only invited me because I was baking his cake."

Shelly looked at her for the longest time. "That's not true. Do you really want to turn up looking hot and sweaty, and wearing slacks?"

Leigh's gaze ran down the length of Shelly's slender frame. She had a point. "Keep an eye on the oven for me. I don't want to burn his cake."

"Don't worry about the cake! I'm going to order a cake from Fellini's. It won't be what he expected, but he won't blame you when he finds out."

"You can't tell him."

"I won't tell him if you leave now, and get dressed."

She had no choice. But Shelly was right, she wanted to look as if she'd made an effort.

"You're in for a treat with the cake," Mackenzie told him. "I shouldn't say much, but Leigh really put in a huge effort."

"I didn't want her to go to too much trouble," Rourke replied. He'd often questioned the wisdom of putting this extra burden on Leigh's shoulders by asking her. He should have known that she never did things by half.

"It looks absolutely beautiful," Mackenzie gushed. "She sent a picture of it earlier, but you'll have to wait to see the real thing."

"I'm looking forward to it, whenever they get here."

"She should have been here by now," Mackenzie said, adding to Rourke's worry. "She had everything planned like clockwork."

"Shelly's gone to pick her up." He tried to sound positive, but with neither Shelly nor Leigh answering their phones, he was growing increasingly worried.

Most of his guests were here now. Even Daisy had come, surprising him, because he hadn't been so sure she would. Angelo stuck by her side for most of the evening.

"I'll call her again," said Mackenzie. "She'd planned to go

home and get changed, and it's possible that she might have had a slight faux pas in that department. I'll let you know what I find out." She stepped away, not looking too worried. He hoped she was right, and that it was only a clothing malfunction that had made them late.

"Relax." Dylan handed him a bottle of beer, but he refused to take it.

"Not yet. Maybe later." He couldn't relax until he'd seen Leigh and Shelly. That elusive sister of his wasn't giving him much information. When he'd called Leigh, she hadn't answered, so he was none the wiser. They were now almost an hour and a half late for the party, and he was starting to worry, despite what Mackenzie had said. Shelly had been excited and Leigh would have had everything ready on time. He knew what she was like. With no news from either of them, he was praying that they'd not had some sort of accident; a car accident, or that one of them had suddenly and mysteriously fallen ill.

"It's your party, yet you look so worried," stated Dylan.

"Who's worried?" asked Reed, walking up to him and holding hands with Jenna.

"Birthday boy," Dylan answered.

"Leave him alone," Jenna replied.

"Thank you." He smiled at her. They had been talking earlier when Jenna and Reed had arrived. They'd been among the first guests, along with Dylan and Merry.

"These sausage rolls are to die for," said Merry, joining the group with a plate of sausage rolls in her hand. She offered them around. "Where did you get them?"

"Roxy made them. She's done all the catering tonight."

"I knew they tasted familiar."

"Merry lives in Roxy's diner," said Dylan, taking a sausage roll from her.

"That diner has been there for years," Jenna mused. "I remember it from before we left Starling Bay."

"Roxy's parents used to run it," Rourke told her.

"Have you tried her potato salad? It's got walnuts and celery," said Merry.

"I didn't see it."

"Come and try some," said Merry, breaking away from the group. Jenna followed.

"They're getting on like a house on fire," commented Rourke.

"Aren't you glad?" Reed asked. "Imagine if our girlfriends hated one another. That would make life hell."

"Sure does make for an easier life," agreed Dylan. "Where's your date for the night, Romeo?"

"I don't have a date for the night," Rourke grumbled, shoving his hands deeper in his pockets. He'd been hoping Leigh would have been here by now, because it was going to take him a couple of hours to warm up to her and have the courage to tell her that he knew. He didn't want to do it the moment she arrived, in case she didn't like the idea of him knowing, and made a beeline for the exit. He didn't want to wait until the very end because he was hoping they might get to spend some time together, discussing things, specifically the 'why' behind her reason to send the love notes in the first place.

But at this rate, he wasn't going to get time to do anything.

"Roxy's food is really good," said Reed. "I wish I'd used her for the Valentine's Day ball."

"Why use Roxy when Olivia had your credit card to run up the bill?" Dylan remarked. Olivia's penchant for throwing parties was well-known. "You can use Roxy for your next party, assuming Jenna's a party animal."

"Jenna's nothing like that. She's pretty frugal, as it goes. Doesn't like to spend much. She's just moved out and rented her own apartment."

"She's not living with Shay anymore?" Rourke asked.

Reed shook his head. "You didn't invite Shay?"

"Is that a question or a statement?" Rourke asked.

"Both," Reed replied.

"I don't even know what she looks like," moaned Dylan.

"I didn't invite her," said Rourke, a little defensively, "because she's not one of my close friends."

"But the rest of your possibles are here," Reed countered, lowering his voice and looking around. They all leaned in. "We met Mackenzie earlier, and Roxy's doing the catering. We've even met your work colleagues, some of whom might or might not be in the running."

"Guys, guys, guys," Rourke said, lifting his head up. "I told you, it's not a priority any more. The notes have stopped. I don't know who it was and it doesn't matter." He had no idea what was going to happen when he told Leigh, and he had even less of an idea about what would happen to their friendship, so he was in no position to tell these guys about her. If ever.

"Shay's the only one you mentioned before who isn't here," Dylan noted.

"Look, Sherlock, there's no mystery here. I didn't invite Shay because she's not a friend, and inviting a friend of a friend," he stared hard at Reed, "was going to look awkward. Don't go reading things into her not being here, and for the love of beer, quit going on about that stuff."

"You're looking pretty uptight for a guy who's supposed to be celebrating his birthday," said Reed.

"I'm waiting for my sister and her friend to arrive. She made the cake, but I have no idea where they are."

"Who made the cake?" Dylan asked.

"Leigh, the woman who runs the bookshop."

"Is she a contender?" Reed asked.

"No!"

"That was a defensive 'No,'" said Dylan, raising an eyebrow. He looked at Reed. "Did you think that was a defensive, 'No'?"

"I believe it was," replied Reed, his tone superficially serious.

"She's baked my cake, that's all! I don't know what you guys are insinuating."

Before they could answer, Shelly suddenly peeked her head out into the living room, and gave him a wave when their eyes met. His heart almost leapt out of his ribcage. "And here they are," he said, surprisingly calm on the surface. "Excuse me."

He made his way to the kitchen and found Leigh with her back turned, and Shelly looking slightly anxious. It wasn't his sister's usual party face.

"What time do you call this?" he asked, half-annoyed and half-joking because he was so relieved to see them. "What?" he said out loud, then stopped abruptly when he saw Shelly's hand signals telling him to stop. She nodded at Leigh, who still had her back turned.

Something seemed to be up with Leigh. Instantly, his irritation vanished. "Let's see it then?" he asked. As soon as Leigh turned around, he could tell that something was wrong. She looked upset. Shelly's earlier warning hand signals made him take notice. "Here you go," she said, her voice shaky. She lifted the lid off the cake box, but the monogrammed box from Fellini's told him everything he needed to know.

"We ended up buying another cake…mine didn't come out right. Sorry."

He glanced at Shelly. She looked as if she'd seen a ghost. "That's okay," he said to Leigh. "At least you're here. As it happens, I quite like cake from Fellini's."

"Great. It's a chocolate one, too. Shelly said you liked those." Leigh forced a smile but he could see right through it, and suddenly he wasn't so interested in the cake. He had a million questions to ask her instead.

"Why don't we get something to eat?" Shelly asked.

"Good idea. Before all the food disappears," he suggested, and hoped to catch Shelly by herself so that he could find out what the heck had gone on.

"Why don't you tell him?" Shelly asked, as they hovered around the buffet table. The feast looked appetizing, but Leigh had no appetite. She felt strange tottering around in these heels, and even stranger in this dress, with its belt snug around her waist, and fitting almost like a glove. Why had she let Mackenzie convince her into 'being brave'?

She wasn't in the mood for a party.

"Aren't you eating anything?" Shelly asked.

"I'm not hungry."

"Have something."

"I'm really not hungry."

Shelly set down her plate and turned all serious, all mother hen. "You have to eat. I know it's not easy to forget what happened but we're here now. Don't let Hank ruin the party for you. Rourke wasn't at all disappointed."

"He was being polite."

"It's just a cake, Leigh. He'll understand."

"I know he will. I'm just disappointed and angry with Hank. I never expected that from him."

"Ditching him was the best thing you did."

"Wish I'd never gone out with him."

"Too late to say that now, but just be glad it's all in the past."

"There you are!" Mackenzie came over, all long limbs and a vision of loveliness. An abundance of curls cascaded over one shoulder. Leigh introduced Shelly and Mackenzie, before Shelly excused herself and disappeared.

"Why so late?" Mackenzie asked.

"I had an accident with the cake."

"What happened?"

She didn't want to burden Mackenzie with the news, especially since her friend didn't know what Hank was like. So she lied. "I dropped it."

"You did what?"

"I dropped it. It went splat all over the floor."

Mackenzie's face crinkled in disbelief. "But it looked so gorgeous!"

"I started to bake another one but then Shelly turned up and convinced me to get ready. We picked the cake up from Fellini's."

Mackenzie clapped a hand to her forehead in shock. "That sucks. You worked so hard at it."

"It's only a cake."

"But you'd been so excited about it."

"It's all in pieces now. I couldn't salvage any of it."

"At least you're here now. And you're wearing the dress! And the heels, you go, girl!"

"I didn't have a choice. Shelly refused to leave the bookshop unless I went home to get changed first. Did you put her up to it?" Her friends might have colluded into making sure she got all dressed up.

"I hadn't met Shelly until you introduced us," Mackenzie reminded her.

"She's just like you. She told me I had to look like I was going to a party, and not the library."

Mackenzie laughed. "She put it more politely than I would have. It's a good thing you've got sensible friends. You look sensational."

She dismissed Mackenzie's enthusiastic approval of her outfit with a weak smile.

Putting the dress on, and slipping on those heels had made her temporarily forget the nightmare of dealing with Hank earlier. She felt out of sorts being here and wanted to go home, but it would look suspicious if she left now, or sometime in the next hour. While she was sure Rourke wouldn't notice if she left, she felt it was her duty to stick around until the party ended.

CHAPTER 32

"What really happened?" he asked his sister.

"Leigh dropped the cake."

"How?" He found it hard to believe.

"I don't know, but she did," Shelly insisted, holding a pineapple and cheese cocktail stick only inches from her mouth. Rourke still didn't believe her. It was the tell-tale vertical line between her brows that gave it away. His sister was trying too hard to look outraged.

"Leigh isn't clumsy, and I find it hard to believe that she'd just drop my cake. And you were gone so long."

"We had to buy another cake. She had actually started to bake you another cake, can you believe it?"

That he could believe. His lips quirked into a smile.

Shelly put down her cocktail stick, uneaten, then walked over to the corner, away from the kitchen. The music from the tent in the yard was still loud. "I'm not supposed to say anything," she hissed.

"It's my party, you can tell me."

She looked around, as if checking to see that the coast was clear, then whispered in his ear. "Leigh's ex came to the bookshop, saw the cake, got angry and jealous and threw it to the floor."

"He did what?" He felt the tension crawl up his spine. Felt his shoulders stiffen.

"That loser ex of hers dropped the cake on purpose."

"Were you there when it happened?" he asked, his voice low, and cold, and calm.

"No. I walked in after. She already had a second cake in the oven by the time I got there. She was determined to make you another one. The first cake was still lying on the floor."

"That's more like Leigh." And yet he was touched that she would even, after a harrowing experience such as that, continue with making him another cake. She must have been scared, and yet she didn't want to disappoint him.

He had to tell her.

All of it.

Maybe not *this*, that he knew what her ex had done, for she had obviously confided in Shelly, but he could tell her about the love notes now, and talk to her in private because he wanted to know that she was all right.

She was here, and therefore fine—to an extent—but he needed to see that she was really okay. And later, after tonight, he needed to do something about that scumbag ex of hers.

He walked around looking for her but got stopped every so often because everyone wanted to talk to him, and he only wanted to talk to Leigh.

He found her sitting with Mackenzie near the buffet tables. "Hey," he said, joining the two of them.

"Hey," they both acknowledged him. He noticed that Leigh didn't have a plate. "You're not eating?"

"I'm not hungry."

He could see how that might have happened. A douchebag ex-boyfriend turning up unexpectedly and getting violent, even if it was with a cake. Thankfully it was just with the cake. He shuddered. There was no telling what a nutjob like Hank could do with enough provocation.

"Roxy's put together the most amazing feast," he said, trying to start a normal conversation.

"It looks splendid," Leigh offered.

"It tastes splendid," Mackenzie said.

"Are you sure I can't get you a few things to nibble on? You must be hungry?"

"I'll get something later," she told him. That was so typically Leigh; she always tried to please. He stopped pestering her to eat then, because he could see how people took her good nature, and her easy-going way for granted. He could see how a pig like Hank might take this to the extreme level. It disturbed him to think that the man might have hurt her in any way. "Can we talk?" he asked, suddenly unable to tread around any longer.

Leigh looked stunned for a moment, then looked at Mackenzie.

He nodded at her "I meant you, Leigh."

"Me?" She stood up a little slowly, as if she was suddenly hesitant.

He saw the shoulder shrug, and behind her caught Mackenzie winking at him, before he led her to the other end of the living room. There were people everywhere, so he grabbed her hand and led her through the kitchen.

"Hey, dude, got any more beer?" Angelo held up an empty bottle.

"Got plenty of beer," he replied, pointing to the barrel of ice, just to the entrance of the tent. "And if that's empty, ask Roxy."

Angelo's lips quirked up into a smile, and before Rourke could escape, Angelo had shot out his hand. "I'm Angelo," he said to Leigh. "I work with Rourke. This is Daisy." As if on cue, Daisy was suddenly standing next to him.

"I'm Leigh."

"From?" said Angelo, expressing interest.

"From the other room," said Rourke, smoothly, and led Leigh out towards the hallway. There was nowhere to go, aside from outside to the tent, but the music was loud there and it would be impossible to talk properly there.

He glanced up the stairs. "Come upstairs?"

"Why?"

"I need to talk to you. Somewhere private. It won't—"

"Somewhere private? Why?" She looked worried.

"It's nothing…" *Seedy,* he wanted to say, because she looked worried. He hadn't thought how this might look to her. "It's nothing like that. Trust me. I can't talk here. Just give me a moment, Leigh, please?" He waited for her reaction, waited to see the anxiety vanish from her eyes.

"Okay," she said, sighing loudly. He climbed up the stairs, and she followed. Upstairs, he opened the door to his bedroom. Wrong choice, if he didn't want to give her the wrong idea, this wasn't the way to go about it, but she'd already followed him in. "It's not what you think," he said, closing the door, hating the idea that she might think he was trying out his Casanova moves on her. She looked uncomfortable, and folded her arms. "What are we doing in here?"

"I don't mean anything by this." How was he going to say it? Where to begin? He scratched his chin.

"Then can we go back down?" she asked.

It wasn't until he saw the fear in her eyes, that he realized how unnerving this might be for her, and then he wondered if Hank had ever hurt her. "I'm not going to hurt you."

"Now you're scaring me."

"No, no. I mean, you look scared. I want to talk to you, away from everyone else, Leigh. It's too loud downstairs."

"What is it?"

"Why didn't you ever tell me?"

She looked confused. "Tell you what?"

"That it was you. You were the one who sent those letters."

"What letters?" For one tiny second, her face lit up in complete surprise. Then she blinked. He stared at her heart-shaped face. He'd never noticed that before. Or her eyes. He'd known they were brown, but not that they were so big and shiny, like glistening marbles. And, hot damn, she was in a dress.

He had to focus to think. "Those letters I told you about." He wiped his hand over his face, feeling a little uneasy because he couldn't tell how she was taking it. Unlike most women he knew, Leigh kept things to herself. He couldn't read her, he could never figure out what was going on inside that head of hers.

"What makes you think it was me?" she asked, laughing nervously.

"Are you still going to deny it?"

"So," she said, her hand flying to her neck, her brow creasing. "You know."

"Yes, I know."

"Mackenzie told you."

"She never said a thing."

She gave a slight shake of her head. "It was … it was only meant to be a … joke. I didn't mean anything by it. I'm sorry."

"Don't be sorry. It was something that distracted me for a few weeks."

"I mean, sorry it wasn't Mackenzie." She blushed now and looked extremely uncomfortable. And then he understood.

"I'm not sorry." He tried those words, throwing them out, waiting for the effect.

"You're not sorry, not at all?"

"Not one bit." He watched her face for the tiniest reaction, stared at her and held the gaze. Her lips parted, as if she was going to say something, but she was going over it. He understood, it was a lot to take in. Especially after the day she'd already had. She hadn't expected this. Her defenses were down, and she couldn't talk her way out of it.

"But why did you let Mackenzie say it was her?"

"You wanted it to be Mackenzie," she pushed back.

"I might have wanted it to be Mackenzie, at one point, for all of one day, but I'm happy it's not her."

She looked up.

"I was thrilled when I found out it was you."

She still didn't say anything, and he knew he had to tell her, try and convince her in some way that he wasn't just a guy who had an easy time of hitting on women. There was more to him. "Where's the fifth note?"

Her brow creased. "Mackenzie gave it to you."

"But it's not the real one, is it?"

Her lips parted. "What makes you say that?"

"Because it didn't begin with the right letter."

Her mouth fell open, and she looked at him in disbelief. "I figured it out the day Mackenzie slipped me the decoy."

"That same day?"

"That same day."

"You've known all this time?"

"Yes."

She stepped back, trying to process it all.

"Yeah," he said, hoping she was having the same reaction he'd had when he'd discovered it was her. "I was going to shred them all. So I lined them all up one by one and had one final read. That's when I saw the pattern. An acrostic poem, sort of, right, Leigh?" Her features softened. "The first letter of each poem, not of each line, spelled out your name."

"I wasn't sure you'd notice."

"I saw the pattern, and when I saw it, I didn't wish it had been anyone else."

Her cheeks turned pink.

"I was kind of glad it was you. Didn't see it coming, I have to admit, but finding out that it was you…was nice."

She looked uncomfortable. "It was only a joke."

"Do you really mean that?"

Her lips twisted, and he hoped it was because she couldn't bring herself to say no and lie about it.

Leigh wasn't the usual type of woman he went after; she was soft, and sweet, and he wanted to wrap her up in cotton wool, and keep her safe. He wanted to protect her, and coax it out of her, the why behind her sending the notecards, because nobody sent stuff like that unless they meant something by it.

He was flattered, for sure, that it had been her. Out of all the possibles that he'd put together on his short-list, finding out that it had been Leigh, had been the best thing of all. And deciphering her name from the love letters had given him a head start.

When she gave him no answer, he said, "I'm still glad it was you."

"You don't mean that," she said, forcing a grin. It was fake, he could see that now, and he understood it, too, even if he didn't really know her that well yet. He had come to know moods and her mannerisms. He knew more about Leigh than he did about most of the women he asked out on a date.

"I do mean that."

They were friends, and they had history; he'd known her for decades. That meant something. But he was seeing her with new eyes for the very first time, at least it seemed like that to him. He had never considered her in any other way because of that history, because he had known her forever as Shelly's friend, and because she'd been with someone else, or he'd been led to believe that she had.

Yet unknowingly, he had sought her out many times during his random visits to the bookshop. He always enjoyed their conversations, liked to run things by her sometimes, get her opinion, like he had with the love notes when he'd first thought it was Mackenzie.

"This is embarrassing," she said, putting her hand to her face, looking down at the floor, looking uncomfortable. He didn't want to make her feel that way.

"Don't be embarrassed." He reached for her hand, but she pulled hers away.

"But I am. This is what kids do in school. I'm a grown-up, I'm not supposed to do stuff like this."

"It was cute."

"See? That's my point. You thought it was cute. That's what people say about their kids, or what kids say about their cuddly toys."

He grinned, because she was so endearing. "Cute isn't a bad word, Leigh. I meant that as a compliment."

She twisted her hands together. "I didn't think this through, any of it." She was talking to herself now.

"What is there to think through?"

"I don't want it to ruin our friendship."

"It won't." But a woman didn't send out those types of cards unless she meant something by them. For all her stubborn insistence that she had sent them to him for a joke, on the spur of the moment, he didn't believe her. People did things for a reason. Leigh sending him those cards 'for a joke' was about as believable as him sending that old dinosaur, Hyacinth Fitzsimmons, a love letter 'for a joke'. It would never happen.

What did he have to do to prove that he liked her? That he wanted to be more than friends?

CHAPTER 33

She had her proof. Rourke had passed her depth test. He might be the flirt and charmer of Starling Bay, but he had figured out it was her all by himself, because nobody knew about the test, not even Mackenzie. He'd read the poems and knew that the fifth one didn't start with 'H'. He had looked deeper and had connected the dots.

He was more than surface level handsome. He had heart. It was silly, maybe, the way she was looking at things, but he'd figured it out, and that meant something.

A man like Hank wouldn't have made the connection. He wouldn't have had the patience to sit and delve deeper. He would have ripped up the notes after a quick glance.

"Where is it?" he asked again. "The final poem."

She rubbed the back of her neck with her hand. "At home."

"Were you ever going to give it to me?"

"I'm not sure."

"Where you ever going to tell me?"

"No."

"So you were going to leave me guessing forever?"

"You wouldn't have been guessing forever. You lead a far too busy life, both socially and work-wise, and you would have forgotten all about it."

"You don't see it as being unfair, teasing me, and then not giving me the ending?"

She hesitated, unsure as to what he was asking. She had wanted to tell him at some point, but when he'd thought it was Mackenzie, there had been no point. That moment had confirmed what she had always believed, that men like Rourke didn't notice women like her. "I didn't mean to tease you."

"It's a good thing I figured it out, then. Otherwise I might never have known. Will you ever show me the last poem?"

She wanted to cringe. Wasn't sure if he was playing with her, laughing gently, or if he really thought she was a loon. Often, she'd wondered what it would be like to be with a guy like him, a guy who ate at the best restaurants, hung out at the nicest bars, a guy who many women noticed—she knew because she'd watched their reaction from behind the counter at the bookshop.

Rourke was a catch.

Only not hers.

"What do you want to see it for?" she asked, letting out a nervous laugh. "I scribbled them down real fast, they're not… they're not meant to be studied. They have no literary worth."

"Granted, you might not win the Pulitzer." His smile sent goosebumps all over her skin.

"Were they really that bad?" she asked, wincing.

"Not bad at all. Your poems made my day, on many occasions. I wish I'd known it was you sooner."

Why? She wanted to ask, but didn't.

"I'm sorry about the cake."

"I'm sorry too, because I know how long you spent on it. It was selfish of me to ask you to make it."

"I didn't mind."

"You already have enough things to deal with."

"But I—"

He put a finger to her lips, that simple motion making them both stop and stare for a long drawn-out moment. A moment that suddenly opened the floodgates of potential.

He touched her lower lip with his thumb. At least she thought it was his thumb, but she wasn't sure because her insides were melting, her stomach fluttering with tiny butterfly-winged twinges.

She heard him let out a sigh. "Do you have any idea how worried I was when you didn't show up? When neither of you answered your cell phones? I knew it was something bad, because I know you, Leigh. I know you would have been on time, I know how much you put into that cake."

"How do you know?" Which of the two had told him, Shelly or Mackenzie?

"That's not important, and before you go and say anything, I haven't seen the picture."

He'd reached for her hand, she only realized that now. She'd been so busy focusing on the sensations in her belly, in the quickening of her heart, that she hadn't noticed when he'd taken her hand. Just the one hand, but it was enough. The warmth, the softness, the reassurance, all from him holding it.

She didn't want him to let go.

"What happened with the cake?" he asked, his voice as soft as butter.

"It fell."

"It fell?"

She hesitated, not wanting to lie to him again, but it was more than that. She wanted to tell him, just because she had a feeling that he might understand. "Hank dropped it."

A fire raged behind those sea-green eyes. "Hank dropped it?"

She nodded. "He came by the bookshop, and then we ended up arguing."

"About what?"

"He didn't like…" she looked up, catching herself in time. She hadn't wanted to mention that.

"He didn't like what?"

She stared at the floor, trying to think of something believable to say. Not wanting to ruin his birthday with the truth. "It's not important."

"It is to me."

He was standing so close to her that she could smell the musky scent of his cologne. "He didn't like what, Leigh?"

"He didn't like that I was baking a cake for you."

"Why?"

He was tunneling deeper and deeper, hell-bent on getting to the root of it. "It can wait. It's not important. We should get back to your party because your guests will be wondering where you are."

"There's something you're not telling me."

She shrugged. Trying to make up a believable white lie was difficult, especially because his closeness to her suddenly made her mind go AWOL. Part of her wondered why he was here, talking to her now when he should have been downstairs mingling with the guests at his party, and part of her dared to wonder whether it was because he cared so much about her that he wanted the truth even in the middle of his own party.

Her gut told her he did.

Her logic told her to ignore it.

"He was angry," she murmured, more to herself.

"At you?"

"He was always angry at me. He was always annoyed about something I did, or didn't do."

"Did he hurt you?"

"He never hit me."

"But did he hurt you?"

"No. He's never been physical."

His eyes blazed. "People don't have to use their fists to hurt, they can do it with their words, Leigh."

A breath escaped from her lips at the truth he spoke. He was so worked up about it that it caught her off-guard.

"It makes me want to punch him to pieces, knowing that he might have done anything to hurt you."

She looked away. "He never hit me."

"Leigh," he said, his voice so baby soft, so gentle, overloaded with concern. "Then tell me what he was angry about."

She breathed in deeply, knowing that she really didn't want to. The smashed cake was bad enough.

When she didn't answer, he grabbed her arms gently, his hands clasping the soft flesh above her elbows. "Was it about me? Did I do something to annoy him?"

"He thought you and I were together. That stuff you said, about the properties and dinner. He didn't like it."

"He was jealous," he murmured, letting go of her hand. "I shouldn't have pushed him, shouldn't have given him ideas." He rubbed his forehead, his face hard then looked at her. "He took it out on you because of me."

"It's done now. You should let it go. I have."

"I can't let it go. It's all my fault."

"You can't change anything, so it's better to forget about it. It's your party tonight, Rourke. You should tend to your guests."

His expression softened. "I should. I will, but I want you to know that you showing up was the best thing about tonight."

The air whooshed right out of her ribcage at that. She committed his words to memory, saving them later for playback.

"I hate what he did," said Rourke, completely unaware of the emotions he had let loose inside her. "You put all that time and effort into making my cake and he smashed it. It's not the cake I care about, I hate that he hurt you because of me and my big mouth."

"It wasn't your fault. He has issues. I've told him he needs to get them resolved. Talk to someone, but he never listened. I should never have gotten together with him."

"I don't know what you were ever doing with a loser like that in the first place." He stepped towards her. "You're beautiful, and kind and caring. And super smart, too. He had his chance. He should have appreciated you when he had you. You deserve so much more. You're the whole package, Leigh."

"Aww, stop it." It was all well and good him saying that to her now, now that he knew what had happened, and he was trying to make her feel better. But he would never understand that women like her never got noticed? He'd never noticed her before; her in her yoga pants, or jeans and long tops and shirts, hair pulled back in a ponytail. She'd only ever been Leigh from the bookstore to him. Everything he'd said to her just now only proved that he was adept at showering women with compliments.

"You don't believe me?" He grabbed her arms again.

That was exactly it; she didn't believe him. "You wouldn't have noticed me had it not been for the love notes. Guys like you are a million light years away from girls like me." She was a homebody. A bookworm, a baker, a people-pleaser. She had no voice. People overlooked her. She was a typical introvert. Rourke was the opposite. The most exciting thing she'd done all year was send out those love notes. It was way out of her comfort zone. That was about as extreme sport as she got.

"That's not true."

Who was he kidding? "That *is* true," she insisted.

Rourke opened his mouth to say something, then paused.

"See," she told him. "You agree."

He pointed a finger at her, his eyes moving as if he was thinking. "No. Not true. You've always been a friend to me. You were right there in front of my face, and I never saw you. You're right, to some extent, I never did, because I was always chasing for the next thrill, but it was you I came to talk to at the book shop, it was you whose opinions I wanted. I just never knew that until recently."

"You came for the cake and the coffee."

"That too, but I came for advice, and friendly banter, and you."

She shook her head, not quite believing what she was hearing. Wanting to, but finding it hard.

"I know that now, Leigh, because the few times I've left there and not seen you, I felt empty, even if I left with my cake and cup of coffee."

"You're just being nice."

"I'm being truthful. You have no idea how happy I was when I found out it was you and not Mackenzie."

"Mackenzie's beautiful. Stunning, you said."

"But she's not you."

This was awkward. She couldn't tell if he was pitying her, or just being extra nice. "You don't have to overdo the niceness, Rourke. I'm glad you figured out it was me, and…what can I say? I sent those cards because it seemed like a good idea at the time. Something out of my comfort zone, a bit of fun. Everything Mackenzie said to you about the cards, that was true, but it was my truth, not Mackenzie's. I had a bad time on Valentine's Day, and Mackenzie's shop was filled with so many breathtaking displays. There were roses all over the shop, and people coming in and buying huge bunches of flowers for their partners. I felt lonely and sad."

"You missed him?"

"No. He was pestering me. Wouldn't leave me alone even though we split up months before Christmas. I tried to block him out of my mind, but when he'd show up in the bookshop, it was impossible to." She had been happy to split up with Hank. She'd felt lonely, though, when everyone around her was making plans for Valentine's Day, and receiving nice cards and flowers. It wasn't Hank she'd missed as much as the notion of romance.

"You need to tell the police, Leigh. I'll come with you if you're afraid to go alone."

She was touched by his words, but didn't want to get him involved. "It's okay, I can do that by myself."

"It's because of me that he went too far this time. I'm to blame."

She knew she had to do something about Hank. She'd read up about these things, done her research online, but she'd hoped that the problem might disappear by itself. Hank went through phases. When she had seen him with his girlfriend, she had been relieved and happy for herself, but felt sorry for the woman. But Rourke had obviously done something to drive him over the edge.

"Does Shelly know all of this?"

"Not everything. She knew he was controlling, but not more than that. I didn't tell her that he was still pestering me."

"Why didn't you say something?"

"To who?"

"To me."

She stared at him, amazed. "Do you think I would ever have done that?"

"I suppose not."

"There you go, then."

"But you pretended that you were with him."

"To put you off the scent."

"It clearly worked." He wiped his hand over his face, "But I caused a whole heap of trouble for you. I didn't keep my mouth shut when I should have, and I made this happen."

"Let's just call it quits," she suggested. "We both made mistakes."

"You didn't make a mistake. Your cards were a distraction I needed at times."

"I didn't mean anything by them."

"Not even a tiny bit?"

How was she supposed to answer that? By lying, partly. "I just thought it would be nice if I stepped out of my comfort zone and sent a card."

"To the guy you secretly had a crush on."

He prompted those words, but she couldn't deny them. "It took me a while to get back to normal after Hank. To feel good about myself again," she said, explaining when he looked confused. "I wanted a bit of fun. Some light relief, you might say. And that's why."

"I'm glad to have been your light relief, but I feel I put your life in danger."

"You didn't. Hank's harmless."

He shook his head. "You keep making light of it, Leigh. It's more serious than you think. I'm only glad he smashed the cake and nothing else. I'd never have forgiven myself if he'd done something to you." He grabbed her hand with both of his, and lifted it to his chest.

A tornado of emotion swept through her as he lowered his head. For a moment she thought he was going to kiss her hand, and her insides tingled and jostled, and got ready to celebrate. She imagined a line going through the label called friendship, but she didn't know what the new label was, and she worried that she was romanticizing it. Making it be something it wasn't.

And then he let go of her hand, and stared at her sheepishly, as if he himself, the Great Casanova, didn't know what to do. "I wish you'd told me about him sooner," he said, his voice sounding strangely ragged.

She hadn't intended to open up like this to Rourke. Hadn't

meant to burden him with stuff about Hank, but it had been a conversation of revelations.

He looked at her, his expression turning soft and sad. It tugged at her heartstrings.

"You shouldn't be upset about any of this," she told him.

"I hate that it was because of me." It sounded as if he cared. It was written all over his face, in his voice, in his eyes. She wanted to tell him it was okay, that he didn't need to beat himself up about it. That Hank was unpredictable, and angry, and he was out of her life, but her emotions were all over the place, and with her thumping heartbeat driving her to distraction, she was swept up in the moment. "It's not your fault, Rourke."

"If he'd done something to you, I would never have forgiven myself."

"Slightly melodramatic statement there, don't you think?" she asked, smiling a little.

"It's been a day of melodrama, sounds like." And then, she didn't know how it happened, but they smiled, and he moved forward, and she found his arms around her. "You're okay, and you're here, and that's all that matters," she heard him say, felt his lips move against her hair. She clung on, tried not to hold him too tightly, but it was strange, this sensation, half-excitement, half-fear. She didn't dare move in case she broke the spell. But he still held her. He didn't have to be here, didn't have to hold her.

Maybe he *did* care, and did see her. "What's lost and not to be found?" he asked.

"Huh?" She stared up at him.

"In your first poem. Lost, not to be found, what does that mean?"

She cringed. It was bad enough writing these poems, but having him now recite them back was excruciating. "Our friendship. If I told you that it had been me, I was afraid that things would change between us. You'd be embarrassed about it, and you'd avoid coming to the bookshop."

He tightened his embrace. "That's never going to happen."

She savored the moment, dared to rest her head against his shoulder again.

"And light?" he asked, "What's light and still heavy?"

"Us," she said, forcing a laugh to dent the pin-drop silence.

"Us?"

"The way we are around one another; joking, laughing, you telling me about your dates. After Hank, you were my go-to. You made things better for me after being with him. Those dark times for me."

In answer he hugged her again. Then she felt it. A light kiss on the top of her head. "I'll never let him do that to you again."

She wanted to ask what he meant by that, but would save that for later. For now, this new sensation of him and her close together was more than enough for her to take in.

"There you a—"

She jerked her head up, as did Rourke and they both stared into Shelly's shocked face. Her mouth opened wide. Her eyes followed suit. And for the next few seconds nobody spoke.

Then she turned right around, and walked back out without saying a word.

They locked gazes. Rourke still had his arms around her, and she liked that he did. She looked up. He stared down. They smiled.

"Tell me to let go, and I will," he said.

She shook her head, her pulse racing at the realization that they were standing chest-to-chest, face-to-face, so close that she could feel his warm breath, smell his scent. Sea breeze and sunshine.

Rourke Halloran had his arms around her, and was staring at her as if he wanted to kiss her. She was going dizzy just thinking about it. But she wasn't ready for that. Not yet. Not now. Not for a while.

"Relax," he said. "I promise not to make a move on you. Just hold you. For now."

"Oh." The man was a mind-reader, too. That made things easier. "How long shall we stay up here?"

"I could stay here a while."

"But Shelly."

His hands slid down from her waist to her hips. "She looked shell-shocked, didn't she?"

"We should go and make sure she's all right."

"She'll be fine," he said, moving his hands away. "And this… is to be continued."

CHAPTER 34

"Where did you disappear to?" Dylan looked at him suspiciously.

"Needed to sort something out about the cake."

"Upstairs?"

Rourke glared at him. "What are you? My private bodyguard?"

"Depends. Do you need one?"

It got him thinking. "That security firm you always use, the guys who've kept an eye on your house while you've been away."

"Yeah?" Reed replied slowly.

"I need someone to have a few words with a troublemaker I know." He was going to make sure that Leigh reported Hank to the police, but it wouldn't hurt to have someone pay the guy a visit and rough him up a little, with words, if not with punches.

Reed narrowed his eyes. "You're being vague."

"Deliberately." Now wasn't the time to discuss such matters. "But seriously, I need someone. It's a favor for a friend, but I don't want the friend to find out."

"I'll send you some names. Roxy's brother, Jackson, sometimes moonlights there."

Rourke remembered the guy even though it had been a while since he'd last seen Jackson. "He's too good-looking."

"He's built like an ox."

"I need someone more menacing. I need the other guy to be scared."

"Who's the guy you want to scare, and dare I ask why?"

"It's best that you don't ask either."

Reed angled his head, his eyes registering interest. "I'll see what I can do."

"Thanks." Rourke watched Leigh over by the kitchen sink. She was talking to Shelly, and he had an idea that sister of his would be trying to get information out of her. He was sure she'd have a thousand questions for him later. And he'd be ready for them.

Only problem was, what was the state of play between him and Leigh now?

His friends had no idea what was going on, they had no clue about Leigh. So if he asked her out on a date, he'd have a lot of explaining to do.

But was this where they were heading, him and Leigh? At a snail's pace, granted. But he could wait. There was no rush.

He had nastier things, like Hank, to think of before then.

"Here," said Dylan, bringing him an opened bottle of beer. "Drink this. It's a magic potion guaranteed to put a smile on your face."

"Seriously, guys, I've had a smile on my face for most of the evening. You must have been so busy with your girlfriends that you missed it."

She had no idea how Shelly was going to take it. Seeing her and Rourke with their arms around each other would have come as a shock, even though, technically, they hadn't been doing anything.

But then, a hug wasn't totally innocent. Friends didn't do that.

Trepidation tightened her belly as she walked into the kitchen and found Shelly tidying up the cups and plates on the countertop.

"Hey," she said, and started to help. Shelly continued what she was doing, making Leigh feel even more anxious. Then she stopped and faced her. "When did it start, you and my brother?" As usual, Shelly went straight for the jugular. Any answer Leigh gave wasn't going to make sense, unless she mentioned the story behind the love notes, and she would rather keep that to herself. "Kind of just now," she replied truthfully.

"Now?" Disbelief echoed in Shelly's voice.

"Nothing's been going on, I swear, and I'm not even sure if there was anything going on when you walked in." But Rourke had said this was to be continued. While she didn't dare to raise her hopes, his vague cliff-hanger left her clueless. Had he meant them holding one another? Or the conversation?

Shelly didn't answer at once, but instead moved the paper plates and cups to one corner. "Now I know why he's been in such a good mood lately, and why he was in a good mood the last time I was here. It was you all along."

Leigh was about to deny this, when she remembered the meal at The Olive Tree. She'd assumed that Rourke had been happy because of Mackenzie. She now realized that he'd known as early as then that Mackenzie had nothing to do with the love notes. He'd known from then that it had been her.

It was highly possible that his good mood had been because of her.

"I didn't know back then," she replied, studying Shelly's expression. "We've never done *anything*. Or talked about anything like that."

"This is something new?" Shelly asked, in a tone which was difficult to gauge.

"Are you annoyed? Would you be annoyed if it was?"

Her friend smiled at her. "Why would I be annoyed? Two of my favorite people getting together? I would be thrilled! I never saw it coming, that's all, and I don't know why you hid it from me."

"Nothing's happened, we're not seeing one another. We were only talking upstairs."

Shelly's eyes twinkled with mischief. "That didn't look like a lot of talking to me."

"We didn't do anything!"

"Next you'll be telling me you were examining his eyes for a stray eyelash," retorted Shelly. "If you like my brother, you should have told me. I don't know why you two felt you had to sneak around like teens."

It was no use trying to explain it to her. Shelly was adamant that Leigh was holding back. She tried again. "We've never had those kinds of feelings before."

"I know my brother," replied Shelly. "He saw you in that dress, looking so glam, and he suddenly saw the real you."

"The real me is the one you see in the bookshop."

"And look what a little bit of effort does," said Shelly, admiring her dress. "Nice outfit."

"Thanks, Mackenzie helped me choose it."

"It did the trick. Rourke's always been fond of you, Leigh. I guess you walking in looking like a million dollars kind of blew him away."

She might have believed this had she not had the saga with the notes and the depth test to tell her otherwise. Even if she'd come in yoga pants and a shirt, she had a feeling that Rourke would have behaved the same.

He'd finally seen beyond the surface, he'd finally seen her.

But she left it at that.

Shelly suddenly stopped what she was doing and lifted her chin up, as if she was listening to something. "That's my favorite song!" she cried. "Come on, we haven't danced yet."

Dancing? *In these heels?*

Why not?

CHAPTER 35

"Where the heck are you?" cried Dyson.

Rourke hesitated, not wanting to explain that he was at the police station. "I'll be thirty minutes late."

"Thirty minutes?" Dyson's voice screeched out loud and angry. "We've got the first of our potential buyers arriving in the next five minutes. You're supposed to show them around."

The Glassmere property. He had completely forgotten. What with the party and everything else that had happened, his Sunday had seen him and Shelly clearing up the mess and then spend the rest of the day recovering.

Now he was waiting for Leigh to finish making her statement to the police officer. He'd gone along with her as promised, but after the sixth consecutive call from Dyson, he'd stepped out of the room to answer.

"Get here in the next ten minutes, or else," Dyson threatened.

It was a veiled threat. Rourke looked through the window of the room and saw Leigh talking to a police officer. He couldn't walk away and leave her, not now. Not after he'd promised to go with her. "I can't make it in ten, but I can definitely do it in another thirty minutes."

"I don't have that long," Dyson replied, testily. "I'm taking Angelo and Phil." He hung up.

Dyson could be a dick when he wanted to prove a point. Rourke shoved his phone into his pocket, then glanced at Leigh through the window as he debated the dilemma. If they sold the property, the commission would be compromised. He walked back into the room.

When he slipped into the seat beside her, Leigh glanced at him quickly. When he saw the look of relief on her face and a faint smile on her lips, he knew he'd done the right thing.

Everything about the day was golden.

It was raining outside, and she'd had a delivery go missing, and one of her sales assistants had called in sick. And she'd been to the police station and made a report about Hank.

But still, the day was golden.

Rourke had gone with her to the police station first thing in the morning. He'd shown up at the bookshop as soon as she opened. When he first offered to accompany her, she turned him down, not wanting to put him to any trouble, but he seemed to blame himself for Hank's behavior, and so she relented.

Looking back, she was glad he'd been by her side. Making that report to the police officer had been daunting. It hadn't been easy, talking about Hank and the way he had treated her, recounting the number of times he'd shown up at the bookshop and made things difficult for her. Oddly, having Rourke by her side gave her the strength to report everything. He'd been there when she had filled out the paperwork and filed it. All she had to do now was wait for a hearing date. Rourke had told her that he would go with her to court, and that he would be with her while they waited for the judge to reach a decision.

That was weeks away, but she liked the idea that she didn't have to do this alone. She didn't want to involve her parents, didn't want to frighten them. Rourke's support meant everything.

Afterwards, she'd been hoping he would come back with her to the bookshop and have a cup of coffee so that they could talk, but he seemed anxious to get back to work. He mentioned something about Dyson not being too happy. That got her worried. She didn't want to cause any problems for him with the job he loved so much, so she told him to go.

He told her he would come by the bookshop later, if he didn't end up working too late.

She held onto that thought, and had decided to give him the last poem:

How hard it beats, my heart with fear,
that you will not hold any of this dear,
Or should I be brave, and fearless and smart,
And be the one to lay claim to your heart?

She slipped the notecard back into the envelope, then hid it in her folder.

Over the course of the weekend, her entire outlook on life had changed. She had experienced the bleakest of lows along with the incredible highs.

So much had happened between Saturday and now that she was left reeling, not knowing what lay ahead next.

Mackenzie had suggested they go out tonight to the Blue Velvet Bar to do a post-analysis of the party. They hadn't had a chance to catch up yesterday because she'd had to come to the bookshop and finish off the things she'd postponed from the day before. Mackenzie was desperate to know what had gone on between her and Rourke. She'd been sure something had happened, seeing that at some point during the night, she and Rourke had been slow-dancing in the tent.

Nothing, besides the slow-dancing, had happened, but girls being girls, Mackenzie wanted a detailed minute-by-minute exposition of the night, and Leigh would be only too happy to give it to her.

Shelly had gone back to New York, and had promised to come back for another visit in a few weeks' time when no doubt she would also demand an update.

It was coming up to closing time, and she was upstairs, tidying up the shelves and giving the floor a final once-over. She sat on one of the sofas, taking a moment to rest and reminisce about the weekend.

Then she heard Rourke shout out for her.

She got up and looked over the bannister. Her insides turned all light and fluttery when she saw him. "Up here," she cried.

But her nerves vibrated like she'd just stepped off a multi-loop rollercoaster ride. Being alone with him at the party had been different. This could be weird, him being here, their usual place to meet. Would they revert back to their usual roles; Leigh from the bookshop and Rourke the charmer? Or would they be the people they had been at the party?

"What are you doing up here?" he asked, putting down his briefcase.

"Learning to breathe again," she said. "Taking a moment."

"Always good to do that," he agreed.

"I was waiting for you," she said, "I wasn't sure if you would come." That was bold, to say it out aloud. She hadn't known if he would come by again today, and yet here he was.

"Waiting for me?"

She went over to the sofa, opened up her folder and pulled out the envelope. She handed it to him.

He looked at it, a small laugh escaping his lips.

"You asked for the fifth note."

He took it silently, opened and read it. She held her breath, worried, and anxious, and embarrassed all at once, waiting for him to finish. It was when his lips curved up into a smile that she breathed out again.

"Yes," he said, closing the note and putting it into his jacket pocket.

"Yes, what?" Her nerves were on edge. He walked towards her. "*Yes*, I hope you will be the one to lay claim to my heart."

She winced. It sounded so trite. So painfully trite.

"It's sweet," he told her.

"You said it was cute last time." She wondered if he could hear the thump-thump-thumping of her heart. It was so loud.

"Cute, and sweet," he said, after pretending to deliberate over it.

"It wasn't always easy trying to get each poem to start with the letters in my name."

"I understand. It's an occupational hazard for a poet."

That brought a smile to her face. "How was work? How was Dyson?"

"Not too happy. I turned up late for this house I was supposed to be showing to potential buyers."

"The Glassmere one?"

"That's the one."

She didn't know at what point he'd reached for her hands, only that her hands were in his. It was effortless and natural, standing here talking about their day. Hand in hand like this.

She squeezed his hands. "That's so important to you."

"Going to the police station was important."

"But what if he fires you?"

"He wouldn't fire me over something like that. I'm his best salesman. He wouldn't fire me."

She was relieved. The cockiness was alive and well.

"Come to dinner with me," he said suddenly. It wasn't a question, or a statement, as much as it was a sexy request.

She stared at his lips, looked up and caught him staring at her. "It's just dinner, Leigh, nothing else, unless…" He'd seen it, the disappointment on her face that she'd been too late to hide. "Unless you want this to be our first date, because, you know, it could be that, too."

"Our first date?" she asked, moving her body away a few inches, praying that her deodorant was still working, and thankful that she hadn't opted for the garlic mushroom pasta from Roxy's for lunch.

His gaze dipped down to her lips, then back to her eyes, and made her feel as if her nerves were belly-dancing.

"If you're feeling up to it, being brave, and fearless and smart," he recited a line from her poem.

Was she?

"I should go change, maybe," she replied, not wanting to step foot inside a nice restaurant with this man, dressed in her yoga pants.

"Whatever you want," he murmured, lifting his hand and brushing a finger against her cheek. He could have touched her with a live wire, for all the sparks it set off inside her.

"I want," she murmured, inching towards him, liking the feel of his skin against her face. "We had things to continue from the other day."

His eyes widened ever so slightly. "What did you have in mind?"

It wasn't the answer she was expecting. She wanted him to take the lead, but the way he stood there, not moving any closer, not doing anything, told her he wasn't going to make a move. And yet he stared at her so intently that he'd set her cells on fire.

"Dinner sounds lovely." She wondered if he would kiss her now, or whether she would die waiting.

"And you want to go home and get changed first," he stated. "I need to get out of these clothes, too."

"Good idea." She blinked. "And then, of course, you'll have to put some other clothes back on," she said quickly.

He laughed, screwing up his face as if she'd said something ridiculous, which she had, because she wasn't thinking straight. "Are you nervous, because you think I'm going to kiss you?"

"Uh, maybe." Yes. Yes, she was.

"I told you, I wouldn't make a move on you, Leigh, until you were ready."

"Don't you want to kiss me?"

"I've been wanting to kiss you for a long time. Ever since I found out it was you, actually."

She exhaled in reply. "Huh."

"But I'm not going to, until you really want me to."

She did want him to. She didn't want that kiss hanging over her head all the way through dinner.

Should I be brave, and fearless and smart. The line from her hastily scribbled poem flashed through her mind. "Then maybe we could get that part over with before. Reverse the order of things."

"Reverse the order of things," he replied, nodding. "That's not a bad idea."

She felt her cheeks burning, partly from sounding foolish, and so unsophisticated, and nothing like the women he usually dated. But before another self-annihilating thought ambushed her, Rourke's lips claimed her mouth. She was lost in the touch of those sweet, sweet lips against hers, the feel of his hands; both cupping her face gently. It was soft, and lingering, and quick.

And it set her heart rate skyrocketing.

"There," he said, taking her hand. "You won't have to worry about that anymore."

He surprised her, because he understood her.

"I've already enjoyed my evening, in case I forget to tell you later," she said.

"Shall we go?" he asked.

"Yes." An entire evening of being with Rourke, having dinner and talking. She had imagined such things in her bleakest days, never thinking they would actually happen.

Truly, everything about the day was golden.

The gentle hum of conversation was punctured only by the noise of glasses tinkling as he stepped into the Blue Velvet Bar. Rourke looked around for his friends and soon found them in one corner of the bar. Reed's back was towards him, and opposite sat Dylan. His friend raised a hand as soon as he saw Rourke making his way over.

It had been three weeks since he'd last met them at his party. Their usual weekly get-together had been postponed due to many reason, but primarily because he'd been so busy at work.

"Talk about the devil, here he is," said Dylan loud enough so that he would hear. Rourke slapped Reed on the back, by way of a welcome, then shook hands with both before sitting.

"We already ordered you a drink," Reed told him.

"Cheers."

"Talk about us two not having time for you," Reed said. "Look who's talking now."

Of course, he'd been busy with the Glassmere property. But once tonight's surprise was unveiled, once Leigh turned up and he introduced her to the guys, they would not believe that it was only work that had taken his time.

Truth was, it pretty much had. Dyson had done his usual and thrown a slight hissy fit when he'd been late that first time, showing potential buyers the multi-million dollar property. He had taken Phil and Angelo with him, but they weren't any good when it came to closing a sale.

Dyson knew that, and so did Rourke.

So he'd ended up with the Glassmere account anyway and, luckily, he'd managed to sell it a few days ago. The paperwork was still going through, but it was pretty much a done deal. That's what tonight was—a celebration, but with Leigh. At some point he'd have to tell the guys that his stay tonight would be short.

In addition, he had also planned a surprise weekend for Leigh and himself in Cape Cod. He'd told her he was attending a workshop in New York, and he'd asked her to accompany him. She had agreed, thinking they were going just on the weekend, and had put people in charge of the bookstore. But they were leaving tomorrow, on Friday morning, and returning on Monday.

It was a long weekend, but one they both deserved. Leigh especially. She needed a weekend away because, otherwise, that woman would spend all her time at the bookstore. She didn't listen when he told her she would burn out, and she seemed incapable of slowing down.

So he'd made the decision for her; a weekend at a luxury hotel, spa treatments, good food, and just the two of them.

He couldn't wait to see her face when he told her.

"Have we really not met since my party?" he asked, even though he knew.

"I've been away," said Reed. "Business trip in Austin, a whole week of it, and you've been busy at your work." He lifted his beer bottle and pointed it at him.

"Had a property to sell. Dyson's a tyrant. It was hard to get away." He took a swig from his beer bottle, and felt the tension in his shoulders slip away.

"You guys make out as if work is everything," said Dylan. "I've had a huge order for vases, and I've made about fifty in the last few days, but you don't hear me complaining about it."

"You're the Van Gogh of our group," Rourke told him. "You'd die for your art."

"I still have to pay the bills," Dylan retorted. "And I still manage to make time for everyone."

"Did Jenna go with you to Austin?" Rourke asked, thinking of the upcoming weekend with Leigh.

"I wish. But no, she didn't. Couldn't, because she works for Hyacinth, and you know what she's like."

"Isn't Hyacinth the female version of Pennington?" Rourke quipped. Reed's stern-faced butler often looked at him with disapproval.

"Pennington has a heart," Reed replied, "If you dig deep enough. Hyacinth never had one."

"Leave her alone," said Dylan, standing up for her. "She's not so bad when you come to know her."

Rourke laughed. "I'll remind you of this when you end up doing the Christmas pageant again this year."

"I'm not doing it again this year."

"Yes, you are." Reed and Rourke replied in perfect unison. Each year Dylan complained about doing the town's Christmas pageant in the town square on Christmas Eve, and each year Hyacinth somehow roped him into doing it.

"Jenna's taking a week off soon because we're going to Montana to see my parents."

"A week? She's prepared to stay at your parent's ranch for a week?" Rourke asked.

"She loves me. She said she'll do it."

"Maybe we should all get together once you get back?" Dylan suggested. "The five of us. Merry's wanted to get you guys over to her place for a while now."

"Sounds good," said Reed. "Might be just the thing to look forward to once I'm stuck at the ranch."

"Stuck at the ranch?" Rourke asked. "Dude, why do it, if it's going to be something you dread?"

"It's going to be a while before my parents come to visit. It was a huge shock, when they last came and I want to make sure they're okay; about Jenna, and me, and the way things happened."

"Good luck," said Dylan. "Get Jenna to call Merry and decide on a date when you guys are back."

A get together would be nice, thought Rourke. And this time he'd have his plus one.

"Do you have anyone to bring along?" Dylan asked him, tuning in like a psychic. Just as he was about to reply, Leigh walked in. It was such perfect timing. His breath stalled in his chest, just looking at her in her strappy sandals and wrap-around yellow summer dress. She'd started wearing dresses more now, he noticed. A couple of guys looked up as she hovered around the entrance. His jaw tightened. "As it happens, I do have someone to bring. Wait for it..." He got up and strode up to her, his hand sliding around her waist as he kissed her on her lips. Her eyes widened in surprise when they pulled apart. "Someone's happy." He'd never done a public display of affection before, but he hadn't been able to help himself.

"Couldn't resist it. You're looking gorgeous and summery," he whispered in her ear.

"You like it?" she asked, smoothing down the fabric.

"I love it." He reached for her hand. "Ready to meet them, properly?" She'd met his friends at his party, but it had been brief.

"I'm ready."

He led her to Reed and Dylan who were staring at him open-mouthed. If only he had a camera to capture their goofy expressions.

"I'd like you to meet Leigh, the owner of Books & Buns. She was at my party, but I'm not sure if you remember."

"Of course I remember. Leigh," said Reed, standing up and taking her hand.

"You made the cake," said Dylan, also now standing. The boys were on their best behavior.

"Wasn't the cake from Fellini's?" Reed asked.

"Let's not talk about the cake," suggested Rourke. Leigh looked at him and laughed. "That's a topic best avoided."

He could feel his friends' staring at him, at them, at this, and he squeezed Leigh's hand, enjoying the moment.

"Sit down," said Reed, as Dylan scooted over to make space for them.

"We can't stay for long," said Rourke, hating to break it to them like this, but the dinner at Fellini's was booked, and he and Leigh were flying off tomorrow morning. She didn't know that part either.

"Why's that?" asked Reed, pointedly. "We haven't caught up in weeks."

"We can stay for an hour, at most," Rourke replied. He knew the hour would kill his friends. They'd have to be polite and not ask too many questions, especially with Leigh around, and he could already see they were dying to speak to him alone.

"So, I guess it would be dinner for six, at Merry's," he said to Dylan.

"Six, absolutely."

"Dinner?" Leigh asked.

"Dylan's girlfriend Merry, you met her at the party, she's invited us all to her place for dinner in a couple of weeks' time."

"I know Merry. She's lovely. She was introducing me to lots of people."

"She was?" asked Dylan surprised. "She didn't know many people."

"She obviously made friends," replied Rourke. "Thank goodness your girlfriend has more social skills than you."

"You're hilarious," replied Dylan, joking.

They ordered more drinks, and talked. Leigh hadn't wanted him to mention anything about the love notes, because she found it embarrassing, and so he didn't, but Reed and Dylan were smart, and he was sure they'd figured it out.

Leigh surprised him. He'd expected her to be nervous, and shy in a social setting; the opposite of how she was in her bookstore, but she was nothing like that this evening. She joked, and talked with Reed and Dylan as if she'd known them for years.

There was a new-found confidence to her lately, and he couldn't put his finger on it. Couldn't determine if it was because the restraining order had come through, and she now had peace of mind knowing that Hank couldn't walk into her bookstore whenever he wanted. Or maybe her recent joie de vivre was down to there being no more secrets between them.

Or maybe it was just because they were good together. Leigh was different; he felt it in his core. She wasn't someone he'd picked up at a bar. She wasn't short-term. There was something strong and solid about them coming together. It was as if they complimented one another, and brought out the best in each other.

She no longer hid behind verses, and he no longer maintained a showy exterior, especially around her. He cared for her, and even though this was new, and unexpected, each moment he looked at her it was as if he was seeing her for the first time, discovering a new snippet about her, unearthing a new mannerism.

When her cell phone rang, she excused herself and stepped out of the bar for a moment to answer it.

Reed and Dylan jumped him like two rabid dogs.

"What the heck was that?" asked Reed.

"This is how you tell us you've got a new girlfriend?" Dylan moaned.

Rourke held up his hands in defeat. "I wanted to tell you guys sooner, but I couldn't find the right moment."

"So you pick a time when we're at our drinks night and you spring this on us *now?*" Reed shook his head, disbelief flashing through his eyes. Rourke could tell he wasn't angry, though. A semblance of a smile danced on his lips.

"Guys, Dyson's owned me for the last few weeks. I sold that house," he looked at Reed, seeing that he'd be most interested to know since he lived in Glassmere. "And I couldn't find a free moment to tell you. This is the first free day I've had in weeks."

"Did Leigh..." Dylan's brows pushed together. "Did Leigh have anything to do with those notes?"

Rourke ground down on his teeth. Leigh didn't want anyone to know, but he could hardly lie to his friends. He shrugged in answer, then, "Yes, but she'd rather keep that between me and her."

"I'll be damned," said Reed, sitting back in his chair. "You're going out with a woman who can pen a poem."

"A poet," Dylan chimed in.

"She's sweet," Rourke replied, unable to stop himself from smiling each time he thought of her.

"I can see you're sweet on her," Reed replied.

"Yeah. This must be serious, if you're introducing us to her after only a few weeks."

He was serious about her, that was why he let his smile answer for him.

Reed's forehead suddenly puckered. "Roxy's brother—the small job you had for him, is that something to do with Leigh?"

"What small job?" asked Dylan, completely unaware.

"It's not important," he said to Dylan," and then to Reed. "It was and that's all I'm going to say about it."

He'd ended up talking to Jackson. It wasn't simple, getting a guy from a security firm to go and make serious threats, but Jackson moonlighted on the side, did various odd jobs, and had his own little security company going. Jackson had gone to Hank's place of work, and had words with him. After that, Rourke breathed a little easier. He would tell Leigh, one day. Just not yet.

"I don't know what to say," Dylan stated. "I don't know if I liked you better when you used to tell us every little detail, or now, when you tell us nothing and everything is a secret."

"This is new. I had to be sure," he replied. "And I didn't want you guys breathing down my neck and asking me a hundred questions."

"Because that's your role, usually, hey, pal?" Reed winked at him.

"We're going away for the weekend," he told them, lowering his voice. "I've booked a beautiful place in Cape Cod. Don't say anything, it's a surprise."

"Definitely don't say anything," Reed said, "This makes me taking Jenna to see my parents seem lame in comparison."

"And definitely don't mention this to Merry," replied Dylan, "because I'm not taking her anywhere. I might try and convince her to cancel that meal, seeing that you two will have come back from your romantic getaways."

"But Forest Heights is a luxury development," Reed reminded him, "You don't really need to take her anywhere seeing that she lives there."

"Merry told me she loves her new apartment, and this new lease of life she's found with you. She said meeting you was the best thing that had happened to her in years," Rourke told him.

Dylan frowned, as if he didn't trust anything that he said. "I'm being serious," Rourke insisted. "I forgot to mention it to you on the night of the party, but that's what she said."

"She might have been slightly tipsy," Reed offered.

"But it's a fact," said Dylan, drawing out a breath. "I don't need to take my girlfriend on a fancy trip or anything, because she's content to be with me no matter what."

"Yeah, yeah, alright, Mr. Romantic," said Rourke, "Just because you can do fancy things with your fingers that none of us can." Rourke's face turned bright red just then because Leigh had returned, and she'd heard his comment.

"He makes things with clay," Rourke explained.

"Oh, I see," she said, as they all collectively breathed a sigh of relief. She sat back down again.

"Everything okay?" he asked, putting a protective arm around her shoulder. He worried about her, because of Hank, despite Jackson's intervention, and the restraining order. She was going to be fine, but still, he worried, because he was falling for her. It made his heart go funny sometimes, miss a beat, jump, and trip.

"It was Heidi. She was asking something about a delivery tomorrow. I don't know why she's worried about that. I take care of the deliveries."

"We should go," Rourke suggested.

"Already?" Dylan looked disappointed.

"We're second in line now," Reed reminded him. "We come after Leigh in his hierarchy."

Leigh laughed. "I did tell him to move our dinner reservation to another day."

"But I've earned my commission," said Rourke, standing up. "And I wanted to celebrate with my girlfriend."

"You'd have thought he'd ask his best friends," said Dylan to Reed. Rourke rolled his eyes at Leigh, seeing that his friends were going to talk about him as if he wasn't there.

"Why don't you both come along?" Leigh suggested, innocently.

Rourke was about to reply, 'No,', when his friends said the same.

"Another time," suggested Reed.

"We'll have you guys over for dinner, just like Merry suggested," said Dylan.

~

"They're nice guys," she said, as they walked, hand-in-hand to Fellini's.

"They're not bad."

"Didn't you want to stay longer?" The last thing she wanted was to get in the way of Rourke's friendship, and it sounded as if he had a good thing with Reed and Dylan.

"No way."

"Are you sure?" She'd told him he was being too adventurous booking their dinner reservation on the same day as he was finally getting together with his friends. but he'd made a huge commission recently and he wanted to celebrate. Who was she to stand in the way of his celebration?

"I'm positive. I booked the table for eight, and I'm looking forward to spending the evening with you for a change."

"Me, too."

They'd both been busy lately, but they still managed to see one another daily, even if it was just Rourke coming to the bookshop for cake and coffee.

She hadn't seen Hank. It had been a few weeks since that last visit, and he hadn't set foot in the bookstore since. Maybe he knew he'd overstepped a line, either that, or the restraining order kept him in line. Whatever it was seemed to be doing the trick.

"I'm starving," she confessed. Mackenzie had been pea-green with envy when she found out that not only were they going to Fellini's for dinner, but that she was going to New York with Rourke this weekend. She'd already made an itinerary of things she wanted to do while he was at his workshop. There were restaurants Rourke booked, and places they wanted to visit, but there were museums and art galleries that she wanted to see, so she'd planned to do that alone during the day.

They stopped just outside the engraved and rather majestic-looking door of the restaurant. "What?" she asked, when Rourke suddenly stopped, and didn't go in.

"We're not going to New York."

"We're not?"

"There's no workshop either."

"No workshop?"

The words sank in, and for a heart-stopping second, she wondered if he was about to dump her, tell her that it wasn't working, that he was bored, that they were better off as friends.

She braced herself, moved her hand away, and suited up in her imaginary Ironman armor. "You've changed your mind, then?" she asked, saving him the trouble of saying it. He was silent, the moment stretching out painfully, like needles in her skin. "We're going to Cape Cod."

"Cape Cod?" she asked, holding her breath. It didn't connect, didn't make sense.

He leaned in, his lips brushing across hers, and sending tiny, tiny, tiny shivers skating across her belly. "We're taking a much needed break, Leigh. Just you and me. We're going sight-seeing, and swimming, and taking things easy."

She released the breath she'd been holding. "We are?"

"You look worried. What don't you like?"

The tender egg-shells she'd been treading on had just given way to firmer ground. Surer footing. "You had me worried for a moment." She dared to smile, feeling something warm flow through her core. "I wasn't sure what you meant."

"A weekend break."

She squeezed his hand, then leaned in and kissed him. This

time his arms wrapped around her and he pulled her against him. The kiss drew out longer.

She was so used to expecting the worst, that she'd forgotten to expect the best. This was more than she had envisaged, her and Rourke and the idea of something wonderful growing from here on in.

And all because of those notes she had penned. She'd taken a chance, moved out of her comfort zone, and in return she'd been rewarded with a man who made her feel worthy.

"It sounds too good to be true."

"It's true, and it's happening tomorrow."

"Tomorrow?"

"We're getting a flight in the morning."

"We are?" But she had so many things to sort out at the bookstore.

As if reading her mind, he tilted her chin up. "I've spoken to Heidi and Larissa. They've got it covered."

He'd spoken to her assistants without her knowing?

This man was too good to be true. She kissed him again, and stared into his eyes, feeling her own eyes well up.

"It's a happy occasion, Leigh." He cupped her face gently.

"I know." She blinked, overcome by much emotion, and hoped he wouldn't make too much of it.

"Shall we?" he asked, moving away and holding the door open.

She nodded, eager to step into a future that looked rosy, for once.

Thank you for reading *Love Letters*!

. . .

I hope you enjoyed Rourke and Leigh's story. I would be grateful if you could leave a review. **A review can be as short as one sentence, and your opinion goes a long way in helping others decide if a book is for them.**

The fourth book in the series, Shay's story, *From Faking to Forever,* is now available.

You can read an excerpt at the end of this book

If you'd like to be notified of new book releases and more please subscribe to my newsletter here:

http://www.siennacarr.com/newsletter

Thank you,

Sienna

EXCERPT: FROM FAKING TO FOREVER

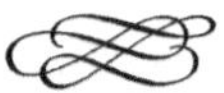

CHAPTER 1

Eight legs. Shay couldn't stop looking at the spider's long, spindly legs, and the mean way he was looking at her. She jumped back. Was it really possible that something so small could cause her so much fear? She didn't like his beady little eyes.

Her heart thumped wildly, because the danger was real.

She reached for her insect catcher, which was always conveniently placed nearby. With the long-handled contraption in her hand, she crawled along the floor, shivering with horror as she tried to trap it in the little compartment. This was the tricky part. The spider crawled away, and she tried again until she finally managed to trap it. She flinched as she stared at it, even trapped, it still felt to her as if it was crawling along her bare skin. "Eww," she winced, rising slowly from the floor, then pointed the bug-catcher out of the window, and released the unwanted intruder.

At times like this she missed having Jenna around. Jenna had no fear of these things. Maybe she was better prepared for them because of her cleaning jobs.

Not that Jenna would ever resort to any more cleaning jobs.

Not now that she was happily dating Reed Knight, one of Starling Bay's wealthiest men.

It reminded her that she still needed to catch up with Jenna because her friend wanted to tell her all about her visit to Montana, a few weeks ago when she went along with Reed to the ranch where his parents lived.

They had been trying to meet up but with both of them busy at work, and Jenna obviously spending a lot of her spare time with Reed, setting a date had so far proved impossible. Plus, with Shay's father recovering from his recent lung cancer surgery, she'd had no free time to herself, and spent the weekends at her parents' place.

At least she'd get to see Jenna tonight with the monthly business owner's social at the town hall. Jenna now worked for Hyacinth Fitzsimmons, Starling Bay's self-proclaimed busybody, and she was responsible for the admin side of tonight's meeting, namely the attendee list and the refreshment table.

These monthly meetings enabled all the business owners to mingle and network. Everyone was welcome, but it was mainly comprised of professional people, most of whom owned their own businesses. Shay and Francine attended every month because it was an opportunity to network and bring in more business for the recruitment company which Francine owned, and for which Shay worked.

She set the bug-catcher down, then brushed the dust off her skirt then noticed she had a stain on it.

Darn it.

She was already running late and Francine was a stickler for her Monday morning meetings. Rushing into her bedroom, Shay pulled out another skirt from her closet, then shimmied out of the one she was wearing when the phone went off. She answered quickly, pulling the new skirt on. "Hello," she said, doing up the zipper as she balanced the phone on her shoulder and tilted her head.

"Is this Miss Donovan?"

It was a voice she didn't recognize. "Yes." She tugged at her blouse from under her skirt so that her blouse was smooth.

"Miss Shay Donovan?"

"Yes." Irritation crept into her voice. "Who is this?"

"I'm calling from Dubois, Barclay and Kleinmeister."

Who? This was different to the usual prank calls she received. She rolled her eyes because this was sucking up time she didn't have, and she was already late for work. "Sorry, I'm not interested in whatever you have to sell." And she hung up.

When the phone rang a second time, she cut it off, then grabbed her handbag and her cell phone, cast her eye over the apartment one more time, her eyes lasering in on the lookout for more creepy crawlies. Finding nothing, she breathed a sigh of relief then closed the door behind her.

CHAPTER 2

Great. Another pregnancy.

Blake, held his head in his hands as Ellen, the latest member from his office administration team, left his office having announced the third pregnancy in the team of four ladies.

This was the last thing he needed first thing on a Monday morning. He had no doubt that Ellen was now happily going around the office and factory floor spreading her happy news, which would take up an hour out of her work this morning.

"What's wrong?" Ralph asked walking in. His general foreman wandered in from time to time. He was in charge of all the operations on the factory floor and reported to Blake. He often offered more than general feedback regarding the day-to-day production details. Ralph also seemed to know everything that went on, and part of the reason was because his wife Nancy headed up the administration office.

At least Nancy wouldn't be surprising him with pregnancy news. She and Ralph had become grandparents for the first time.

"Ellen's pregnant."

"You didn't have anything to do with that did you?" Ralph asked him, chortling at his own silly joke.

"Do you really think?" Blake didn't intend to finish the sentence. For a fifty-something, happily married man, and a recent grandfather, Ralph was supposed to be the voice of reason. Sometimes Blake looked to him to bounce ideas off, but sometimes, like now, the guy could come out with some silly things.

"I blame the office chair," Ralph chortled. "You need to get it replaced. I swear each time one of those women sit on it, they get pregnant."

"You'd better hope that Nancy doesn't sit on it," he threw back, folding his arms with satisfaction at the worried look on Ralph's face.

"We've just become grandparents for the first time. I assure you, Nancy won't be announcing any such news now, or ever. But you…" Ralph pointed a finger at him. "Isn't it about high time you got your head out of your computer and met some nice young woman? It's been a while since you did any of that."

"Women?" Blake snorted. No thank you. Callie French had been the last woman he'd dated, but that had been over a year ago. He'd been pleased when it had ended. They both had.

"You can dismiss it all you want now, but you're going to end up old and lonely if you don't do something about it soon."

"I'm not interested in doing anything about it soon," he growled, needing to get on with his work.

"And who are you going to pass on this company to?"

"Just because you've had a grandchild, doesn't mean you have to lecture to me about offspring."

"I could always hook you up with my niece. She's around your age and gorgeous. I'd rather her meet a decent guy than try any of these dating websites."

Not the niece again. Blake sucked in his breath. "Thanks for the compliment, but no."

Ralph planted his hands on his hips, and looked down at him. "Let me guess, you've been here all day and probably most of the night too."

Blake didn't reply at first. He did spend a lot of time here, but he also went home to get changed and showered. Still, he was doing twelve to fourteen hour days, easily. This business took up his life. It wasn't easy running a factory which manufactured rubber flooring tiles as well as luxury vinyl tile for residential and commercial use. It was a small floundering company when he'd bought it a few years ago, but he'd managed to get it back on track and make it profitable. Ralph and Nancy and most of the employees had stayed on when he took over, but he had expanded considerably in a few short years, to the point that the expansion was leaving a hole in his profits, and the business was taking up all of his time. He didn't have the time or the energy to think about women.

"And what if I did?" he asked, finally.

"Did you do anything this weekend? Go out, meet any people, circulate, have a social life? The chances of you meeting a woman are less than my chances of losing any weight." He patted his potbelly with pride.

Blake stared up testily. "So what if I was here all weekend?" He was the one whose neck was on the line. He was responsible for the wages of his employees, not Ralph. Not anyone else. He sat back, placed his hands on the back of his neck, and pondered his latest problem. "Three pregnancies," he muttered. "Why now? Why all at the same time?"

Ralph chuckled. "It happens, especially if you're happily married."

While he was happy for those who were happily married and pregnant, this didn't bode well for his business; even though business was booming and sales were increasing every single year.

It was a great position to be in, but it would put a dent in his business because he needed everything to continue to flow. He needed three able replacements for the women who would go on maternity leave.

On top of that, he'd recently had some renovations done, a new outbuilding for storage, and had plans to expand the factory floor some more. He was trying to rein in his expansion, as he knew this could cause potential problems further down the line and he didn't want to grow too fast, then fizzle out and die. Slow and steady was his plan, but random things out of the blue continued to give him financial and logistical headaches.

"I need three replacements in the next six months." Dionne and Penny had announced their pregnancies a few weeks ago, and Ellen just now. That was three quarters of his admin team gone. Poof!

"You can talk to those fine ladies from the recruitment agency," Ralph suggested, with a wink. "Seeing that you've got that meeting tonight."

True. He was attending the monthly meeting at the town hall. Lately, these were his only social outlet, and he found himself looking forward to them.

He would speak to Francine and Shay. They were nice and he'd had plenty of business dealings with them in the past. They were the answer to his short-term employee problems.

Things were suddenly looking a little brighter.

He wasn't averse to seeing Shay Donovan. She was practical, and down to earth, and quite easy on the eye. He found her endearing, and funny. There was nothing romantic between them, but a love-hate dialog often ensued when he spoke to her. He found her endearing, always pushing up her spectacles, and coming out with some funny comments, and this was as much as he could handle right now.

No romance, just a pleasant and friendly encounter. Nothing more.

From Faking to Forever is available at all retailers.

BOOKLIST

Whirlwind Kisses
Winter's Kiss
Maid for Him
Love Letters
Escape to Starling Bay (Books 1-3)
From Faking to Forever
Winter's Vow
Guarded Hearts
Table for Two
A Bouquet of Charm
Christmas Hope

For a complete list of books go to:
http://www.siennacarr.com/books

ACKNOWLEDGMENTS

I would like to thank my amazing group of proofreaders who check my manuscript for errors, typos and inconsistencies.
I am eternally grateful for their help and support:

Marcia Chamberlain
Nancy Dormanski
April Lowe
Dena Pugh
Charlotte Rebelein
Carole Tunstall

I would also like to thank Tatiana Vila of Vila Design for creating the awesome cover.

ABOUT THE AUTHOR

Sienna Carr is the sweet romance pen name for an author who has been writing romance since 2013. She lives in the UK with her husband, three children, and a parrot.

Connect with Me

I love hearing from you – so please don't be shy!
You can email me at: sienna@siennacarr.com

Copyright © 2019 Sienna Carr

Love Letters (Starling Bay, Book 3)

This is a work of fiction. All characters, names, places and events are the product of the author's imagination or used fictitiously and do not bear any resemblance to any real person, alive or dead.